MW00572742

ALSO BY TOMAS MONIZ

FICTION
Big Familia

NONFICTION
Rad Dad: Dispatches from the Frontiers of Fatherhood
co-edited with Jeremy Adam Smith

ALL
FRIENDS
ARE
NECESSARY

ALL FRIENDS ARE NECESSARY

a novel by

Tomas Moniz

ALGONQUIN BOOKS OF CHAPEL HILL 2024

Published by
Algonquin Books of Chapel Hill
Post Office Box 2225
Chapel Hill, North Carolina 27515-2225

an imprint of WORKMAN PUBLISHING
a division of HACHETTE BOOK GROUP, INC.
1290 Avenue of the Americas,
New York, NY 10104

Acknowledgment is made to the following, in which parts of this book first appeared, some
differently titled or in slightly different form: Mason Jar Press, *All Friends Are Necessary,
Part 1*; *X-R-A-Y Literary Magazine*, "Like a Needle to Record"; *7 x 7 LA*, "Who Doesn't
Like Bubbles?"; *Pine Hills Review*, "The Tenderness in Books and Friends"; *Santa Fe Noir*,
"Life Cycle of a Fern"; *Lost Balloon*, "Balls and Stars"; *Catapult*, "Every Homie Needs a
Nickname"; *Peach Mag*, "The Baby."

Printed in the United States of America.
Design by Steve Godwin.

Library of Congress Cataloging-in-Publication Data

Names: Moniz, Tomas, author.
Title: All friends are necessary : a novel / by Tomas Moniz.
Description: First edition. | Chapel Hill, North Carolina : Algonquin Books of Chapel
Hill, 2024. | Identifiers: LCCN 2024005155 (print) | LCCN 2024005156 (ebook) |
ISBN 9781643755816 (hardcover) | ISBN 9781643755830 (ebook)
Subjects: LCGFT: Novels.
Classification: LCC PS3613.O528 A79 2024 (print) | LCC PS3613.O528 (ebook) |
DDC 813/.6—dc23/eng/20240307
LC record available at https://lccn.loc.gov/2024005155
LC ebook record available at https://lccn.loc.gov/2024005156

10 9 8 7 6 5 4 3 2 1

First Edition

To Zakiyah
again, again

Divine am I inside and out, and I make holy whatever
   I touch or am touch'd from,
The scent of these arm-pits aroma finer than prayer

—WALT WHITMAN

CONTENTS

PART THREE

ALL
FRIENDS
ARE
NECESSARY

PART ONE

Summer 2018

The Body Is a Wild, Wild Thing

EVERYONE LOVES THE Conservatory of Flowers in Golden Gate Park, understandably so, with its glorious and cocky tulips, its vibrant rhododendrons and azaleas, blooming all year despite the season. But I'll take the earthy floor under a California redwood, especially today: a miserable ninety-five degrees in the city. I'm avoiding all my responsibilities by biking through the park, seeking shade under the redwoods, surrounded by their accompaniment of green ferns. Give me the obviously sexist-named lady fern, fronds all delicate and bendy, and sword fern, with fronds erect and plump. The moist smell of decomposition. The coolness. The occasional pile of trash: Takis bags, cigarette butts, a mini bottle of Don Julio tequila, the makings of a perfectly fine evening. Which reminds me— tonight I'll be celebrating my thirty-seventh birthday.

It's early afternoon on the summer solstice, the longest day of the year, unnaturally hot, and soon I'll be meeting my best friend, Metal Matt, at Bender's on Nineteenth and Van Ness to drink. Then we're going to jump in the Pacific Ocean.

That's the plan.

My beat-up Bianchi, which Metal Matt lent me, sprawls a few feet away, and I lean against the tree trunk. I enable my hot spot, hoping not to exceed my data this month, because I'm still on a shared plan with Luna, my ex-wife, who continues to pay the bill. I need to find a more permanent job and living situation. I secured two temp jobs for the summer: a library assistant at Cal, and a data entry position at MOMA, because though the pay is nothing special, you get free access to the museum.

Metal Matt keeps telling me to look for a place to live in Oakland. It's cheaper, warmer, more bikeable. For now, I've found a sublet on Shotwell and Seventeenth in the Mission till September. Nearby: a BART stop, a spin studio, a grocery store, and a bar. I've decided to quit drinking for the summer—after tonight, of course—so I should just cut the bar, but it's psychologically comforting to have so close.

I click open a new tab and decide to peruse the Craigslist Missed Connections. I chuckle at the ridiculousness of the postings. The earnest longing. The raunchiness of anonymity. But they arouse something in me, something romantic and hopeful, perhaps a little desperate as well: *You, in line at El Farolito, wearing a Pink Floyd shirt, with a date who acted disinterested in you. We stared at each other for a long moment. Me, in shorts and shirt and gym bag and very interested in you.*

I have this wish that I'll read one about me: *You, a healthy and young-looking 30-year-old, maybe 220, clean-shaven, with a dark and wildly curly head of hair, biking laboriously but joyfully around the city. Me, someone who thinks you are adorable.*

But apparently no one misses me.

I scroll through a few ads for shared apartments in the city, but I can't focus, overwhelmed by how quickly plans can change. I lived with Luna for over five years in Seattle. We'd purchased a set of Heath dinnerware for the kitchen, Ikea plant stands for hallways. I'd painted our unborn child's bedroom a soft daffodil that we picked out after bickering for weeks over subtle variations of yellow paint swatches.

I know I'm not really ready for roommates or communal chores.

A cat sticks its head out from behind a lady fern. Long-haired, all whites and tans and blacks, slinking along the perimeter of the tree's circle of shade as if I've taken its spot. It circles me like something feral and then stops and rudely stares. I never had a cat growing up, so I'm a little suspicious, but there is something wonderful about a warm furry thing curling up on you. I try to call it over, but it just sits there all regal-like, its tail twitching, continuing to stare. I stare back but then blink. The cat wins, looking at me like *You're pathetic,* and immediately Luna pops into my head, which disturbs me.

Our breakup wasn't for a lack of love or friendship or passion. We had fun. We dreamed and planned about the future. Even pregnant, we role-played. We confronted our fears about how our lives might change with a child: nanny and parent, needy neighbor and pervy neighbor, ignored mom at the park and dirty father sitting next to her.

I haven't been with someone since Luna, since the day before she left for the doctor's office. I not only miss sex with her, but all that came with it: the way I could lose myself, act ravenous or demure, find such direction, such purpose, in pleasing.

Something in me loves the feeling of letting go—of *Tell me what to do,* of *Anything you want,* of service.

I tsk-tsk and say, Kitty, come here.

The cat doesn't move. Typical.

I ignore it and begin to pack up, and the cat walks right up to me.

I'm a sucker for success and stroke its sides, rub its belly, and the cat meows, then rolls over and scratches me with its back legs and bolts away.

I watch blood pop up in little lines along the soft underside of my wrist. Three perfect rows. I reach down and lick them tentatively. Consider the taste of my blood on my tongue, the viscosity. It's not as thick as cum but thicker than pre-cum. A bit sharp to the taste but definitely different than period blood. I lick again and it beads, and I lick again, and it continues to bead. The body is a wild, wild thing.

I gather my belongings together, reluctant to leave the shade under the trees, but I want to be among people and need to bike back to the Mission. The crowded sidewalks of the park on a busy summer day. The designated roller-skate area, a large asphalt rectangle, bumps with sweaty and shirtless men.

I straddle my bike and watch the synchronized routine of four women practicing circle eights together. The requisite aging San Francisco hippies, sporting dreadlocks and tie-dye shirts, taking up too much space. Normally, I'd shake my head, but something's lovely about it all. The joy, the pleasure, the shared spaces and slick bodies and lack of any kind of pretension.

An old man, also watching the show, on what appears to be a stolen Citi-Bike with a milk crate affixed to its front with a series of bungee cords, suddenly tumbles to the asphalt, and people rush to help him. He gets up, refuses their concern, yelling that he's fine, he's on his birthday bike ride—he's on his way to Ocean Beach.

I smile. I want to yell, *That's my birthday plan too!*

A woman keeps asking him, Who's the president? and he says, That asshole.

I hear someone shout, He's fine.

I watch kids learning to ride bikes or scooting around on skateboards, elbows and knees covered with pads. Some parents hover over them, running beside them, shouting directions, voices full of fear or concern. Some parents stare at their phones like they are thankful for the break from paying attention to a child, not even reacting when they fall. The kids look awkward and ridiculous but alive, skating and falling and getting back up. And it hits me viscerally, like a punch. I can taste the bitterness in my mouth, feel the anger in my body, at the unfairness of loss, at expectations and hope and possibility taken away, just gone.

I drop the bike and pull out my phone. I text Metal Matt: *I'm heading to the bar earlier.*

He immediately texts back: *You good?*

I text the dancing emoji.

He texts the peach.

He knows me well.

I feel my shoulders drop, feel air fill my lungs.

After almost a decade together, Luna and I haven't spoken in months. We text here and there. To check in. To perhaps remind ourselves of one another, of what we had together. The desire to connect still feels instinctual.

I decide to send her a preemptive birthday text: *I hope you doing well. Letting you know I'm fine & w/ friends.*

Luna texts: *I know. I'm glad.* And the lit candle emoji.

I gave her so much shit for her candles and altars and brocade runners, her rituals around solstices and anniversaries, special votives accompanying intentions and manifestations. I teased her that my hippie white mom had altars. She never bit.

Luna would reply, Good for her. People need more spirituality in their lives. But hippies don't own the practice. They never have. I'm simply reappropriating.

Then I realize she knows my plans. That she and Metal Matt probably still talk to each other. That he updates her about me.

My phone buzzes. It's Luna, so I decline it.

She texts: *Be well, Chino.* Then a heart emoji and then a peach emoji.

I notice she avoids the word *birthday.*

I understand why, of course.

The heat hangs on everything as I leave the park and head down the Wiggle toward the Mission, always grateful for this bike-friendly path flowing through the heart of San Francisco. I cruise slowly but determinedly, taking up the whole green bike lane as other cyclists squeeze by, ding-dinging their little bells at me to make space.

I refuse to budge.

So that's why I'm irritated as I wait patiently at a light astride my borrowed bike, helmet on, earbuds in, at Sixteenth and Van Ness, when this '70s red Bronco decides to make a right turn and beeps at me. I looked at him like *Fuck you.* He waves through the windshield for me to get out of the way. I pull my earbuds

out and roll my bike back, eyeballing him like *Don't beep at me.*
I realize he's an elder: black Ray-Bans, white tank top, dangling
gold chain, and one of those mid-'90s Mossimo red flannels,
unbuttoned. He looks like my father or my tios back in New
Mexico. He rolls slowly beside me, window down, raising his
hand, calming me, and says, Bro. It's okay. It's okay.

I feel frazzled and foolish. A bad combination.

That's the mood I'm in as I lock my bike up and enter
Bender's, hearing the familiar melodic sound of Black Sabbath,
a kind of divinity, a beautiful darkness, the familiarity of home,
all dirty and smelly but yours. I decide to splurge on Pliny the
Elder, which is in its own way something divine: flowery and citrusy and malty-sweet. I grin and ask for a Pliny and slap down
seven bucks. The bartender smiles and tells me, It's eight.

I only have eight: seven for the beer, one for the tip.

Metal Matt promised to spot me drinks for the rest of the
night. To cheer me up. To kick off my summer of sobriety in the
right way. Now I'm an asshole again, the guy who's not going
to leave a tip.

I say, I thought it was seven.

The bartender's like, That was months ago. Things change,
my friend.

I say, Here's eight. When my friend comes, I'll tip you.

Right, they say. And walk away.

I hurry to the outdoor patio to get out of sight. I place my
beer down on a stunningly nasty glass tabletop that hasn't been
wiped down in weeks and keep my phone in my lap. The ash-
tray, however, looks like it gets cleaned regularly. A single big
table made of an old wooden door takes up most of the patio.

The group of people sitting around it appear familiar with each other and they're all dressed in shades of black. I'm sporting my only pair of swim trunks, horizontal pastel stripes hanging to my knees, and a plain black T-shirt. So I'm only slightly out of place. No one looks my way. I watch them pass a pack of smokes around. Everyone grabs one. They pass around a lighter between the three women and two men. The men all sport leather vests and tight black denim shorts, fringe dangling down, tickling thighs that appear taut and tan. The women lean back in their chairs, wearing T-shirts with the sides cut out. I try not to stare at their unshaved armpits and the lovely way their whole bodies move as they laugh. They blow smoke directly into each other's smiling faces like it's an act of love.

I sip my beer and notice these other two dudes sitting at the only other little circular table, in the corner sharing a bowl. And by *dude* I mean the complete opposite of the old man in the car or the black-clad people at the big table. One's wearing a Hardly Strictly Bluegrass shirt with gray sweatpants and what appear to be house slippers. The other wears khaki pants, socks with sandals, and what might be the matching top to the gray sweatpants. The dude with the shirt sees me looking and says to me, Got to love Pliny.

I'm speechless. I look at the beer: brown, a bit reddish, with a small head of foam.

I want to ask how he knows it's Pliny and not one of the other thirty beers Bender's has on tap, but instead I say, You like Pliny too?

He says, Man, I got a story for you. He leans forward and offers me the pipe. My first instinct is to say no. But it's my birthday. I lean in, and he leans in with the pipe and lights it with his blue plastic lighter. I inhale.

Hardly Strictly Bluegrass points the pipe at my beer and says, The brewery is up north. It's this packed sports bar. Like you'd never want to go in there. Like they have fifteen-dollar hamburgers, and fries are like five extra dollars. But here's the secret. If you ask them *Is the* Child *around?* they'll give you a mini pint of Pliny the Younger if they have some. It's never advertised. You just have to know what to say. You have to have faith. Have you ever had the Younger?

I've never tasted the Child, I say, trying to be clever. But the word triggers me: *child*. My body surges with a rush of sadness, my skin flushes, my belly turns.

He says, It's just like heaven.

One of the women at the larger table stands to leave, and Hardly Strictly Bluegrass sees her and says, Sorry 'bout that, milady. Like he's in eighteenth-century England. He watches her leave—not in a douchey way, but still. I look to the sky, dull now with night coming. I breathe out slowly, audibly, but I don't care. I sip and savor my beer. I sense my body unclenching, my heart calming. I'm ready to go to Ocean Beach, which I expressed must be the final destination of the evening.

Metal Matt used the word *kismet* when I bragged to him about my plan on the phone the day before.

I asked, What the fuck is *kismet*?

He said, It means like fate or destiny. It means everything led you to be in this place with this opportunity.

I said, A birthday is hardly an opportunity.

He laughed loudly, like I was ridiculous.

I asked, And what language is that?

He said, Yiddish or Hebrew, I think. I don't know. I'm not Jewish, but I'm one spiritual motherfucker. All true metalheads are. Remember that.

❧

AND LIKE A miracle, Metal Matt enters the patio holding two PBR tall boys and a huge white hibiscus flower. He makes eye contact with me and states loudly, Drink up, and let's get nude and jump in the ocean. A woman from the larger table behind us yells, Metal Matt! Where you been?

He says, Being a good boy and living in Oakland. Then Metal Matt says hello to everyone at the table, and I hear one of them say, The beach sounds like a good idea on a night like this.

Metal Matt says, It's a special night. It's summer solstice, it's hella hot, and it's Chino's birthday.

They all look at me—the men, the women, Metal Matt, the two dudes in the corner. They all wish me a happy birthday, their voices a jangle of sound. Metal Matt makes his way to me and hands me the beer and the hibiscus.

I say, Thanks for the flower. A hairy-fruited hibiscus.

I tuck it behind my ear.

He says, Hairy fruit, are you serious? I love it.

Metal Matt strokes his red beard, bushy, a bit unkempt, beginning to gray right down the middle. He has long reddish-brown hair perfectly parted in the center. He takes care of it. We were roommates for years, and the amount of money he spent on hair products was impressive: shampoos, hair conditioners, oils, rehydrating creams.

We crack open the cans and cheers each other as white foam flicks onto my sleeve. He shows me a fifth of Maker's from his back pocket and says, I'm saving on beer so we can take a Lyft to the beach.

I say, A sentence I never imagined coming out of your mouth.

He says, Yeah, well, I never thought Slayer would say some reactionary conservative drivel, but whatever, right?

I say, Who knew Ozzy would star in a reality TV show?

Hardly Strictly Bluegrass joins in: Or that Metallica would play the Super Bowl?

And he's so pleased with himself I have to chuckle.

Not Metal Matt. Metal Matt restrains himself and says curtly, They played a concert the day before the Super Bowl that was only slightly connected to it.

Hardly Strictly Bluegrass says, Right, right. And does the smart thing and turns away toward his friend.

✹

IN THE LYFT, later, Metal Matt says, Happy thirty-seventh birthday.

I say, It's the last prime birthday of my thirties.

Metal Matt says, Did you know thirty-seven is the exact number of seconds of recorded bells and thunderstorms during the opening of the song "Black Sabbath" on the album *Black Sabbath* by the band Black Sabbath, which as you know marks the birth of metal, a holy moment. How's that for a trifecta? You and Black Sabbath.

I put my hand on his and squeeze it.

The Lyft's radio is playing KFOG, and on comes Metallica's "Nothing Else Matters." It's somber and slow and picks up and crunches in that perfect power-ballad kind of way.

I say, Kismet.

And Metal Matt says, No. That's just eerie as fuck.

The driver turns it up. We sip the fifth during the rest of the drive into Golden Gate Park. We say nothing else as I watch the silhouettes of California redwoods and invasive eucalyptus against the clear, starry sky. No ocean fog at all.

When we get to the beach, we walk hand in hand till the moment the dry sand becomes wet. We strip naked. People gather and sit in circles here and there. Some have fires, some play music. Nothing I recognize. It's surprisingly calm for Ocean Beach on a solstice evening. The waves lap the shore. At first, I worry that people are watching me, that my belly bounces like a beach ball, that my dick hides away in my pubic hair. Metal Matt absolutely never wears his hair in a bun, but he puts it in one. I watch as he calmly wraps his hair around and around. He doesn't even turn to look at me, just mutters, Don't even say it.

Then he says, We're going to sprint into the water.

I say, Not too far. There're riptides.

He says, There always are.

He says, We're going to yell and scream the entire length of this beach. I want you to let everything go.

I say, Oh. Just like that. Should be easy.

He says, Nope. Easy is staying on the shore. Right here. This is going to be hard.

I say, No one else is swimming.

He turns, naked, to face me.

I say, I get it. I need to move on. I need to get over all the shit that's happened. To leave it all behind me.

He shakes his head no and says, Chino, I really don't know. Maybe someday. But tonight if you want to be brave, do something that scares you.

I say, This is an example of being brave?

He says, It can be.

He then hustles back to his jeans and bends over, and I see the glow of his pale ass cheeks and the darkness between. He returns holding the bottle. He opens it and takes a swig. He hands it to me. I finish it off and hand it back. He then tosses the bottle in this exaggerated, celebratory way. Then he yells to someone behind my shoulder, Relax. I'll pick it up in a second.

He looks at me, Fucking liberals. We hug, his warm chest and belly pressing into mine. We turn to face the ocean. I hear him breathe in deeply and then growl, low and guttural, picking up intensity and sounding as beautiful as early Neurosis or Metallica or any damn Sabbath album pre–Ronnie James Dio. I join in. And there is no harmony, no syncopation, just long, drawn-out noise, unbroken and off-key.

And then we run.

I WAKE THE next day to the sound of banging on the door to my street-level sublet. But the only thing that comes to mind: *Day one of sobriety.* Not: *Am I safe? Is there a fire? Do I need to evacuate?* Because no one should be able to access my door from Shotwell unless they jumped the security gate. I feel proud of myself as I welcome the sense of purpose that comes with a boundary: no drinking for three months. I see it's twelve thirty in the afternoon and realize it has to be Kay and Mike at the door for our lunch date that I'm not at all prepared for.

Kay enters holding three foil-wrapped burritos stacked in a perfect triangle in her hands. Mike enters behind her carrying a disposable drink tray with three large Coke cups. He looks at me and sips from each paper straw.

Mike says, To avoid any spillage.

Kay says, Metal Matt said you might need a delivery. And PS—your gate was wide open, with your bike just sitting there.

I have a moment of *How did I get home last night?* panic and feel even better about my sobriety summer.

Besides Metal Matt, they're the only other friends I made at SFSU. Kay aspires to write in her time away from preschooling. She has short brown hair and a lot of energy. Mike freelance copyedits for several tech companies and brags to each of us that he loves his job.

Kay pushes me backward, saying, Sit, sit. Let me plate these birthday burritos.

I say, I might need some coffee first.

Mike sips from one of the drinks and says, Trust me, get some food in your belly first. Then coffee.

He sips from a different straw, holding eye contact, grinning.

Gross, dude. Give me one of those.

He sits next to me and places the tray on the ground in front of us.

Mike puts his hands on each of my shoulders. He looks like he might say something, but instead pulls me to him. At first, I stiffen, but I close my eyes. I relax into it, and it feels good. To be held.

Kay must enter because I hear, Ahhh, men hugging is a wonderful sight.

I try to remember the last time I was hugged: Metal Matt on the beach last night, but not really anyone else for a while. This jolt of energy rushes through me: *When did Luna last hug me?* I can't remember. It must have been the day she left. I think of my father—I hugged him in his home in New Mexico. My mother: I hugged her on her hospital bed, and she patted me on the back.

That was the final time I would touch her. She would pass away the next day. I was eighteen. When I saw her body, I didn't go near it.

I open my eyes just as Kay leans in for a group hug. I don't resist. I let her. I let them hold me. No one has to say a thing, but of course Kay does. She's always been a talker.

I'm glad you're back home. It's been too long since we've seen you.

And then we part, and together we unwrap burritos. Kay and I carefully, deliberately peel back the tinfoil halfway down like normal people. Mike frees the entire burrito, balling up the tinfoil like an animal.

I say, This is the last gluttonous meal I will eat.

I tell them about my decision to be sober and eat healthier.

Mike says, Spoken like a man who drank too much the night before.

I say, I'm serious. I need a cleanse. A new beginning.

Kay says, You have my support.

❦

I NAP FOR the rest of the afternoon, and when I wake, I strip and shower, then remain naked as I curl up on the couch. I contemplate jacking off. I consider scenarios or situations that might pique my interest: MMF three-ways usually do the trick. And lately I've been such a sucker for reluctance plotlines: People who know they shouldn't but just can't help it. Friends at parties. Strangers stuck in precarious situations. Coworkers in the breakroom. Even exes.

But nothing hits right.

I wonder if my cleanse should involve porn. It's way too easy. It takes no work. No agency. No creativity.

I pick up my phone and see the last missed call from yesterday: Luna.

I have this rush of wanting clarity and closure, this need to accomplish something.

There are a few things I still have to resolve from my life in Seattle: the phone-bill issue and the storage locker that Metal Matt and I quickly filled with remaining belongings Luna and I owned, all the stuff she didn't know what to do with as she left for her parents' house, leaving all of it—including me and our marriage—behind.

I sit up and hit CALL.

She answers on the third ring.

I hang up immediately and put the phone down.

I want to say *I miss you.* I want to say *I'm sorry about how things transpired. I'm heartbroken. I'm lonely. I'm angry.* I want to ask *How are you doing?*

Instead, I text, *Hey, I realize we need to deal with the phone contract.*

I text, *I can PayPal you money once I get settled* and a thumbs-up emoji, as if that's the end, as if there is nothing more I need to say to her about it. I know she hates when I just make unilateral decisions, but I can't help it. And I hate myself for not being about to do something different. Better. Mature.

I stare at my phone. The three little dots appear. I watch them blink, eager, anticipating.

They disappear.

She never responds.

Like Needle to Record

I'M RIDING BART to West Oakland to meet Terrance for the first time, and I'm practicing my small talk in response to those generic first-date questions.

Terrance is hopefully a new friend. A very sexy friend, according to Metal Matt, who orchestrated this meet-up, a.k.a. blind brunch date slash possible hookup.

Metal Matt believes I need a safe yet physical distraction.

He knows my history with men and women, having lived with me as I tried to figure all that out. One night right after college, I complained about a date being uncomfortable with me also seeing a woman. We were on BART headed to 924 Gilman to see a punk band from LA we read about in *Razorcake*.

He said, Why do *you* need to figure anything out? Seems like you have. Seems like *they* need to figure something out.

The way he phrased it felt so obvious and clear. So easy.

The first generic question: *What do you do?*

I was a biology teacher in Seattle for years.

Yes, I do miss my students, but I absolutely do not want to return to a school district. I want to work with kids and talk about trees and plants outside, not in a classroom. I blame Ms. Frizzle and *The Magic School Bus*, which I watched constantly as a child, for leading me to a degree in botany at SFSU and then a career teaching middle school.

I always lined my classroom desk with cacti and succulents, and through the year we'd vote on imaginative new names for the strangest plants.

Kalanchoe, which students couldn't touch because it's toxic, we renamed Nacho Cheese Doritos. The kids laughed at *Sedum rubrotinctum* and agreed the common name for it was already perfect: pork and beans.

My poor aloe vera plant was continually decimated by Timmy C, because I happened to explain to him the medicinal benefits of the plant on cuts. Every few weeks he offered proof on various appendages for a new aloe leaf to help him heal.

I love the sound of children screaming *Mr. Flores*.

So my answer to the question What do you do?: Call me Mr. Flores, eighth-grade science teacher extraordinaire.

Generic question #2, usually about my name: *So, Chino Flores is interesting.*

My actual birth name is Efren, after my grandfather, a big, kind man everyone loved and who gardened, ate voraciously, and died peacefully in his sleep of heart failure before I was two. But I go by Chino. My father started calling me Chino because my mother spent her pregnancy in Shenzhen, China, on a "Women in Math" exchange program. My dad told everyone after I was born that I looked like a cute chinito, with black hair and little eyes, that maybe I wasn't his.

But despite the implication, my mother loved it, whispering it to me in those quiet moments: *My China flower.*

The times I saw my father during my childhood, he never called me Efren, always Chino. I never thought twice about my name until my mother defended it in front of me to a school administrator who suggested that I be addressed by my *real* name.

What do you mean? my mother asked.

Not a nickname, he said.

What's the problem with his nickname?

It's inappropriate.

Chino?

Yes, to refer to someone as China or Chinese because he may appear Asian. I won't let any child be teased for their appearance.

We call him that because I spent my entire pregnancy in China. He's my little China flower.

Which leads to generic question #3: *So where are your parents?*

My father: we are in contact, but barely.

My mother passed away when I was eighteen, almost twenty years ago. Before that, we moved constantly. In fact, I envy her ability to just pick up and leave everything behind: apartments, jobs, men—a strength there I could use right now.

But Terrance doesn't ask a single question.

He greets me at the door with a smirk.

My goodness, Chino, you look a little nervous.

I shift my weight to one foot, and say, Please, trying to sound absolutely not nervous.

But I can't hide it. Even I can tell I'm pretending, that I feel eager and skeptical and awkward.

He says, Come, come—and ushers me into the middle of his studio apartment. He then points to the record console and says, Sit and choose a record. I'm making us food. I want to feed you. And he retreats to the kitchen to make us healthy lunch bowls, like we do this all the time.

And Metal Matt is certainly right. Terrance definitely distracts: mixed race and husky, wearing lightweight and breathable yoga pants tight in such interesting places and a loose cropped shirt with the sleeves cut off, revealing the underside of his belly. He moves through the kitchen area in plaid house slippers.

The way he's dressed, I can tell he's not planning on leaving the house, so I slip off my Nikes and I plop down on the plush carpet, happy to focus on choosing the music.

But I struggle. I don't want to offend. The predominance of '80s pop stupefies.

The closest thing to metal I find: Bon Jovi. I figure, *Sure. Why not?* I pull the album from the shelf.

I say, How's this? And hold the sleeve high so he can see.

He's constructing our bowls of quinoa and garbanzo beans and swiss chard (easier to digest than kale, I'm informed), real bacon (for him) and tempeh bacon (for me).

We're both trying to get healthy. No booze. No wheat. No drama.

I don't miss the wheat or the drama. But come nighttime, I usually do miss the booze. It's been two weeks.

He doesn't look up but says, Doesn't matter.

I say, Honestly? Everyone always says that, but really?

He says, If I own it, I should have no problem hearing it.

I say, I agree.

But secretly, I don't. There's times I want something specific— the long hard buildup of doom metal or the fast punch of thrash.

Everything matters.

I pull the record out, and it has this plastic sleeve that crinkles and bunches. I can't imagine trying to slide it back in. I figure I'll deal with that particular stress later and place the album on top of the turntable. The needle moves, and the speakers crackle to life.

But it's not anything remotely like metal. This poppy drumbeat races, and a guitar joins, and immediately it picks up speed and energy, and I instantly recognize it. All I can do is bob my head.

Suddenly, Terrance races in from the kitchen with wooden salad tongs, pretending that it's a mic, sliding in his house slippers across the floor like he's done this a million times. He belts along with Belinda Carlisle of the Go-Go's—*See the people walking down the street*—and it's the silliest, most beautiful thing ever.

I say, This is definitely not Bon Jovi.

He smirks but says, I'm so glad you found it. I've been searching for this record.

I say, You have? And realize I sound so dismissive, so judgy, and he's so cute.

He says, Sometimes, what you need finds you.

We got the beat, he sings. And I pick it up: *We got the beat.*

I sit cross-legged on the carpet and smile up at him. I must look some kind of way, because he says, Let's dance.

He reaches his hand to me, but I don't take it. I stand on my own accord and say, It's like ten thirty in the morning. I'm not only sober, but I haven't even had any coffee.

He says, You're afraid you can't dance because you're sober and uncaffeinated?

He says this as if he's a bit disappointed in who I am. He stares at me. He's still holding the tongs up to his mouth. Like he's hungry. I look at his outstretched arm, notice a group of small geometric tattoos at his elbow crease.

I say, You want me to dance to *this* song?

He says, What would you like?

I worry he's placating me, but whatever.

I say, Not the '80s.

He says, Fine, rolls his eyes and kills the music, lifting the needle. I feel a moment of sadness as the song ends. He steps to the laptop on the coffee table and flips it open.

He says, How's this playlist: Cali Love. Don't ask what's on it. Let's just find out together.

I shrug, like *Of course,* but can't help looking. I step to the screen and read some names I know: Joni Mitchell, Missing Persons. But then I see Mac Dre and Andre Nickatina's "My Homeboys Chevy." I click on it. Dre starts talking about getting *your weed from the store the legit way.* Dre says, *Quit thuggin' out.* Terrance and I both bounce our shoulders to the beat.

Then Terrance dances. And I dance. We keep two feet distance between us, and then I reach a hand out and he reaches a hand out, and we touch. Like needle to record. Like voice track to drum track. Like *Welcome home* and *Stay a while*.

The Tenderness in Books and Friends

THE FOLLOWING SATURDAY night, Kay and Mike and I stand in the back at this literary reading in the Mission, because Kay fidgets too much and Mike is so obvious when he gets bored that it's embarrassing. Me, I could care less. I'm here to be with them and to have something to do, so I don't sit alone in my sublet pining dramatically for a drink or binge-watching episodes of some dumbass Marvel show. Luke Cage punches away the boredom, but come on.

The bookstore has this section of books and zines focused on local interests, right next to where we stand. I see this one called *Literary SF: A Foldout Map*. I open it, and there are pictures of ten white dudes and one woman placed at various locations across the city, but the main focus is on North Beach and the Beats. I have trouble folding the map back up and feel the person at the register staring at me.

I say, You guys. Check this out.

They both look, and I hold it up like evidence.

Kay says, I bet it's all Beat poets.

She brushes her short hair to the side.

Mike whispers, I hate Beat poetry.

Mike always sounds like he's whispering, but he has a great laugh, with his stocky body flexing like a fist with each chuckle.

I say, Me too, but then I remember some Ginsberg poem with a line about shoulders and wheels and not giving a fuck anymore that I must've read in an undergraduate English survey course. I remember reading about him with men, with women, all kinds of friends, and community and drugs and sex. I remember wanting something like that.

This older guy wearing a red baseball hat proclaiming MAKE AMERICA MEXICO AGAIN looks back at us from his seat and says, How can you not like the Beats?

He looks at Mike.

I think he's jesting, but there's an edge to his comment. The lady next to him shushes him and looks back at us like we're guilty too.

Mike whispers even more hushed than normal, Damn, not only did we get literally shamed, but we also just got literarily shamed. Get it? Shamed . . . literarily.

Mike uses actual air quotes when he says *literarily*, like we actually might not get it.

The bookstore worker who watched me trying to fold the map calls me over. She's midthirties, wearing a white cable-knit sweater low enough to reveal a chest tattoo: the head of a dragon.

She says, We noticed the same thing. We even looked for another publication to supplement this one but couldn't find anything.

I say, You should talk to Kay and Mike about it. They're the English majors.

Not you? she asks.

Definitely not me.

Let me guess: business.

Ouch. How dare you. Biology. I especially love ferns.

I give her a look, and she smiles.

Kay nudges Mike and says, Who would you add?

Mike says, That's hella easy. You want classic? How about Oscar Zeta Acosta from right here in the Mission.

The worker says, What did he write again?

Mike playfully flinches.

Kay says, The whole '90s spoken-word thing exploded here.

I say, Unfortunately.

All three frown at me like *Fuck you*. I frown back at them.

The event happens to be selling red cups of foamy Lagunitas about four feet from me. I don't really want to drink, but something in me feels bereft. I haven't craved a beer this bad in a while. The person pumping the keg is half-assing it, and every cup is half foam and half beer. I can't look. I just can't.

One of the readers announces her piece with an epigraph by Ginsberg. She reads from her poem about bodies and freedom and refusing to be silent. I clap at the end. We all do. It's a beautiful, creepy poem, and I want to stretch my neck to the side because part of me wants to see what she looks like, but part of me knows that's not the point.

The awkward mingling begins. People are weird. I'm not Mr. Gregarious either, but still.

Kay and Mike are doing their schmoozing. I move through the crowd to get by the front door so I'm ready to bounce. Mr.

Baseball Hat is there. He looks at me and says, There you are. I had an idea. You all should make your own guide to new literary things in the city.

He says it like I should thank him for the idea.

I nod and say nothing, because why?

He slaps my shoulder and leaves. I turn back to the store, and the worker in the cable-knit sweater grins at me and says, He means well.

I say, I'm sure he does, but still.

She nods. I nod. We both smile without showing any teeth. I feel stupid, so I finally say, What's your name?

She says, I'm Leila.

I say, I'm Chino.

She's closing up and stacking heavy boxes of books, which appear to be full of hardback novels with splashy, colorful covers.

She tells me like I asked a question, People keep dropping off donations, or if we don't buy the books they bring, they just leave them, as if they're doing us a favor.

I ask, Are they worthless?

She says, Not really, but we focus more on the literary arts. These are more bestsellers and mass-market paperbacks, so we send them to Goodwill. You want a box?

Before I answer, the event's curator announces they'll roll the keg to the new park a few blocks away and invites the audience to come finish it.

Leila says, You should meet me there.

She stares right at me and doesn't flinch.

I say, I will.

Kay and Mike want to go home, but I hear myself plead, Let's get some sparkling water and head to the park.

Mike looks around and sees Leila watching us.

Mike says, Does someone have a little crush?

I feel juvenile. I'm about to disagree, but he grabs my hand and says sincerely, And that's a good thing, Chino.

I say, I just had a date with a handsome fella named Terrance.

You can always have more dates.

I walk away from him, but I have to admit to myself that I do desire attention. The uncomplicated, soft kind. Usually, I find that easier with men, but something about this bookseller's toppy, direct energy entices me.

At the park, people stand in little circles, a perfect summer evening. The park's name is in Mayan: In Chan Kaajal, meaning My Little Town. A song by E-40 is blaring from a music cube hanging from bike handlebars. The song's about drinking straight from the bottle, and it's in these damn beautiful moments I wish I still drank. I smile, thinking of Terrance and dancing, remembering the moment we touched hands, then wrapped arms around waists, then kissed. And though it stopped there, it was all so joyous, so simple.

They need to kill the keg quickly, because Our Little Town closes its gates in thirty minutes. Kay and Mike banter on about the Mission landmarks they'd feature if they could redo that map of literary San Francisco. They list: Modern Times Bookstore. Dog Eared Books. The Mission Hotel.

I ask, What's up with the Mission Hotel?

Mike says, Are you being serious? Acosta wrote like all of *The Autobiography of a Brown Buffalo* there. Don't make me pull your Latinx card.

I say, I'm a botanist. Why would I read about buffaloes?

I try to hold a straight face but can't. We laugh. Mike, his body pulsing inward. Kay pushing Mike and then me and then Mike. I still try to act like I don't know what they're laughing about. Shrug my shoulders. Tilt my head.

I feel happy.

I see Leila and wave at her like I'm expecting her, like it's a date.

Leila walks up and joins our little circle, and we all stop talking.

It's awkward, but I revel in the desire I feel to make her comfortable, welcome.

I say, They were just talking about how they'd redo that literary map.

I gesture to my friends. I say, Leila, this is Mike, and this is Kay.

She says, That's a good idea.

Mike says, It is, but I want to do something more practical.

Kay says, More practical than a book?

Mike says, A book tucked up on some bookshelf? I mean, if you don't read, like homie here, and he points at me.

I read, I shout.

I push Mike gently, and he steps back, acting like I shoved him.

I look at Leila.

I softly say, I read.

She whispers, Good for you.

But that smile she gives me makes me want to thank Mike for his comment.

Mike continues, Okay, so I'm glad you read, but if you

don't generally read, are you then going to read a book about writers?

No one responds, because what's to say?

Leila says, Stencil something at each spot.

Kay says, I like the way you think.

Mike immediately proposes we do it now.

He says, Chino, you live like two blocks away from the Mission Hotel. Don't you have a box cutter and some spray paint?

I say, I'm subletting. I don't know what I have. But Walgreens is close.

All four of us take up the whole sidewalk walking to Sixteenth, like wild animals. We score some cardboard from a pile of recycling on the way and brainstorm what to stencil. We decide on BROWN BUFFALOES LIVE / READ ACOSTA. We also try to come up with a cool acronym for our clandestine literary cell. The others quickly dismiss Bay Area Literary Society (or BALS) as a superbad idea, but I love it. We bum-rush the drugstore's office supply section under extremely bright lights. The only color spray paint they have is emergency orange, locked behind a glass partition. We wait ten minutes to get someone to open it.

Walking back, the fog begins to push in over the hills from Ocean Beach. We pass tents where people are living along Folsom. Back at the park where we all met, In Chan Kaajal, cops harass a few people who've refused to leave at closing time. We quietly approach the Mission Hotel on South Van Ness.

There are two people gathered just outside the front door, a man standing and a woman in a wheelchair. I know what a single-room occupancy hotel is, but I've never actually been in one. None of us have. I feel a bit embarrassed and privileged—always a bad combo.

Kay and Leila roam the entrance for a potential spot to emblazon our literary manifesto. Mike and I enter the lobby. The concierge, an elderly man, well-dressed, in a crisp bright flannel, sports the bushiest silver beard I've ever seen. So impressive I wish Metal Matt could see it.

He says, Can I help you?

Mike whispers, Hi. I'm Mike, and this is Chino. We wanted to know if we could put a stencil on the sidewalk in front of the building, commemorating Oscar Acosta, who wrote an important book in this building.

The concierge responds in a way that implies he's not really in the mood: I'm Bill. Nice to meet you. And you mean the brown buffalo dude.

Mike looks right at me like *See, motherfucker.*

Bill says, Look, I don't want to know anything else. Do whatever. But donations are always welcome, if you know what I mean.

We walk out and I tell Kay and Leila, We can do it, but we should leave a donation.

I start straightening the few dollars I have on me.

Leila says, Hold on a second. I have an idea. And she walks into the lobby.

The woman sitting in the wheelchair wearing a black Giants hoodie asks, So is the book good?

Kay answers, because she's been talking to her: I loved it. It's got some problems, though.

The woman says, But what doesn't?

We all nod.

She says, I wonder what room he was in. My room's got a writerly vibe.

The other person, a young guy who shifts back and forth from one foot to the other, dangling his cigarette from his mouth, takes a broom from the entryway like it's been waiting there for us and starts sweeping the sidewalk right in front of the doors. He says, Do it right here.

The glow of the hotel lobby illuminates the pavement like a spotlight.

The woman says, No. Do it on the side of the building. Walking on the guy's name is hella disrespectful.

The concierge's voice crackles over a speaker, Do not spray-paint the side of the building. Miranda, please.

The woman, named Miranda, yells, I'm playing, and looks at us and laughs with her mouth wide open and her tongue sticking out. We give the two-person crew all the money we have.

Leila comes back and says, Let's go do one thing first.

The concierge's voice bursts from the speakers again, And when you come back, bring that book.

We briskly walk back to the bookstore, Leila and I right next to each other.

I feel something like pride as we match footstep for footstep the entire way.

She opens the bookstore door with her keys.

She looks at us and says, It's good to be the manager.

She gets her car from around the corner and double-parks in front as we pass box after box of books from one person to the next, filling the trunk and the back seat.

Kay says, All these have to be worth some money.

Leila says, Hopefully. I told him to give them to tenants to sell and wrote down a few places that might buy them.

Kay and Leila start to cut the stencil and struggle with letters *a*, *b*, and *e*.

I hear Kay say, If we do all caps, it'll be fine.

Leila says, Who knew this would be so hard?

Mike opens one of the literary maps on the counter and writes *Acosta Lives* and the hotel's name and address in black Sharpie. I watch him do the first one with surprisingly perfect penmanship. He puts it back and grabs the rest.

I step into the photography book section. Alone, I touch the spines, glossy and thick, announcing name after name: Arbus, Eggleston, Mapplethorpe, Woodman. Names I remember from my college days, like Ginsberg. I grab book after book and flip to random pictures. Freaky kids in the park in the '60s. The desperate beauty of suburban spaces. Bullwhips in assholes. Black-and-white blurred self-portraits. The tenderness in each person's photos slays me. I hear the sound of my friends' voices encouraging each other. Laughing. Talking about books and the things they love.

Back at the Mission Hotel, we all gather in a semicircle at the entrance. Mike kneels down and places the cardboard on the concrete, and Kay shakes the can. The clack-clack-clack from the spray paint echoes across the street. The woman in the wheelchair calls the young man over. The eight of us—including Bill the concierge, who emerges from the lobby—clap as Mike pulls up the cardboard. There, in the brightest orange imaginable, harshly lit by the hotel foyer, is our commemoration.

Bill grabs the stencil and says, I'll hold on to this for the future.

The woman looks at Mike and says, I love orange—I'm a Giants fan. What're you planning on doing with that spray paint?

Mike says, Nothing. Absolutely nothing. And he hands it over.

Anonymous Armpits and Desire Paths

IT'S LATE JULY, and I've spent the last week BARTing back and forth between the city and Berkeley. I have to ride BART right at the highest commute times to get to my temp research job at Cal. I'm like the worst kind of commuter, with my bike and a coffee mug. I say, *Excuse me, excuse me,* as I slide onto the seven forty-five train to Richmond. I have to ask like ten people to move so I can place my bike on the bike bar. Then I stand holding coffee in one hand, and with the other, I desperately try to reach for the closest hand grip. Two options: reach above or reach to the side. It's all about distance.

I feel most comfortable reaching out to the side, but snaking an arm between strangers' bodies is disconcerting, if also slightly titillating. So I hold on to the bar above, but then I wonder if they can smell me. I examine a forest of arms around me, reaching up. I can't help but stare at armpit after armpit as people sway, their muscles firm and erect, gripping the overhead bar or hand grip. I discover deodorant balls and sweat marks, and hair and stubble. It kills me. The undeniable humanity we all share: the primping, the shaving, sweating, stinking. The possibility of all this intimacy, all this temptation combined with the unbearable reality that I'll never stroke or sniff. Never nuzzle my way along their bodies.

Clearly, I need to get naked with someone. I haven't in a while. A very fun dance/cuddle session with Terrance, with our next hangout coming up, and a date planned with Leila: these have potential, but I'm still reticent. Maybe it's nerves. Maybe I'm just not ready to be vulnerable about desire and my body and the way I like to feel consumed and ravaged. The way I want someone to hold my face in their hands and demand I look at them.

Metal Matt tells me not to stress. To masturbate as often as I want. To flirt in public. To trust my boundaries as necessary for my healing. I don't think about sex with Luna much anymore. I do think about how strange it is that I was married, monogamous, and preparing for a child, and now I'm single and appreciating anonymous armpits. Metal Matt never really dated. I once believed maybe he was asexual, because he never appeared to desire sex. He was just himself. I envied his confidence. His groundedness. The way he prioritized friendships.

He had one girlfriend on and off a few years back, but since then, nothing serious. I'm actually a bit jealous, because Metal Matt acquired a dog, named Sabbath—a chubby, squat pit bull mix, whose tongue always hangs to the side and who's always drooling. Sabbath also has to bark at least one time at every new person or animal he sees. But he's cute, and he cuddles with

Metal Matt on his couch, and that kind of joy makes me want to experience that tenderness, that care again.

This morning on the seven forty-five Richmond-bound train, I enter and try to place my bike, but a group of young women and men in matching brown hoodies with airbrushed lettering across the back stand in the way. They have a little mobile speaker and a stool, and they wear their backpacks hanging from the front. I have to hold my bike in one hand, my coffee with the other, and then stand balancing with the movement of the train. I try to rock with the sway, the push and the pull, knowing most people will get off downtown over the next few stops, and they do.

At the last city stop, the young men keep the center of the car clear from new passengers.

One sees me struggling, and he says, Let me take that for you, mister, and you can put your bike here. He reaches for my coffee.

I say, Mister? How old you think I am?

I hand him the cup.

He says, Age doesn't matter, sir. I respect my elders. And he ushers me to the bike rest area. I thankfully lean my bike and take my coffee back as the music starts. One of them says, Slap that shit. His friend announces, Ladies and gentleman, don't mean to disturb you. We're just trying to make a little money by doing what we love. This is my cousin Richie.

Richie starts to dance. He smiles. He shifts his arm up and over his head in a way that seems impossible. The wrong direction. It pops out of socket and back in as he spins on one leg. He reaches up to the overhead bars and swings to the ceiling and somersaults back to the ground.

It's impressive what the dancers can do in such little space. No hitting passengers, no freaking tourists out or irritating commuters. They laugh with each other. They encourage each other. They tease the one who misses a move and drops his hat. By the time we hit West Oakland, they're walking the aisles, sliding past passengers, smiling and saying thank you, collecting dollar bills. They all disembark, and I watch them gather on the platform and hand the money to Richie, who shoves the wad in his pocket. No one counts the bills or straightens them or anything.

I spend the morning collating research data about patron usage at the university's thirty-two libraries: busiest hours, floor access, areas of interest like journals, computer banks, study rooms, book stacks. Right before lunch, I email the results to Brad and Sandra, my supervisors, who look like tech workers, always moving quickly, sporting puffy North Face vests. Brad, five minutes later, walks into my cubicle, shaking his head, holding his computer tablet. He says, Chino, nice work. I appreciate the clarity. It's just so obvious, right?

I say, What is?

He says, That periodical usage in the library keeps plummeting.

I nod.

He smiles and adds, Bodes ill for that collection. Can't wait to show Sandra these facts. I nod again, not sure why. He walks away like he's proved something.

At break, I follow the sidewalk through the empty campus to find lunch. The majority of students won't return for a month, and half the administrative offices are still closed. I stand just inside and above Sather Gate, the entrance to Sproul Plaza, on one of the small hills that undulate across the campus. The sidewalks curve and slope and crisscross ahead of me. There are groves of native oaks and a huge group of eucalyptus trees, both beautiful.

I observe the shortcuts pedestrians have etched across the grass connecting one path to another. *Desire paths.* A phrase that has stuck with me since Luna and I binged the podcast 99% *Invisible.* They explained: despite what planners envision, people choose their own way, so forward-thinking designers consciously wait to decipher what direction people want to go, then lay out pathways.

I get a text from Metal Matt: *It's Fri. You hanging out w/ Terrance or Leila?*

I text back: *You just want to know if I've had sex yet.*

Metal Matt: *Actually no. I wanted to know if you wanted to go to movie.*

I text: *I'd rather have sex. But fine.* Then I sent the okay emoji.

Metal Matt responds: *7:30, the Roxie.*

I eat my burrito, which is where my desire took me, with precision, folding the crinkly tinfoil slowly down with each bite. I ruminate on Brad telling me *Nice work,* but somehow I feel dirty about it, and not the good kind of dirty, which makes me think of the good kind of dirty. So I find myself fantasizing about sex with Leila or Terrance. Or, better yet, Leila *and* Terrance. Which leads me to imagine informing my friends Metal Matt, Kay, and Mike about having sex, because they worry about me, which I realize makes me feel safe and cared for and probably much happier than any kind of sex could provide.

I text Metal Matt: *Can I invite someone?*

Metal Matt texts: *Of course.* Then the smiley-face emoji.

I text Mike and Kay, but they're busy. They're having a *date* date. They text that they love me. They tell me: *Text SOMEONE?? so you can have a date date.*

I text them: *Stop saying that. No one says that.*

Then I text the smiley poop emoji.

I text Leila: *I know we have coffee plans, but want to be my date to a movie tonight with my best friend? 7:30, the Roxie.*

She texts: *Is this a date date?*

I don't know how to respond.

She then calls. I answer.

She says, I actually hate texting when making plans.

I say, That's fine. I generally hate talking on the phone, but you're an exception.

She says, Great. Compromise is the basis of successful relationships.

I fail to respond, because I immediately wonder what compromises Luna and I could have made to remain successful, to stay together. I wonder if any relationship can ever be successful. I know Metal Matt would say something like: All *relationships are successful, but that doesn't mean they all last forever. Each one produces something worthwhile, some kind of lesson.*

Leila then says, But let's not get ahead of ourselves. I just like to be direct. Is this a serious date, or are you wanting a friend?

I sit in silence for a second. I say, Can it be both?

She says, It can. I'm just not available for anything serious right now. I feel I need to say that. What's the movie?

I say, I actually don't know.

I spend the rest of the afternoon collating numbers for another campus library, but I attempt to make it possible to draw different conclusions. I try to find ways to make things more equal, more balanced. I want to prove Brad wrong and save the periodicals. I discover that library holdings located close to the bathrooms are frequented more than other holdings. I conclude that the flow of patron traffic determines collection usage.

I send this info only to Sandra and not Brad.

At 5 p.m., I bike through the campus to BART. I jostle for position after making people move from the bike area. They stare at me all irritated, like I'm a nuisance. I just smile at them. I choose to extend my arm to the side and grab the bar. I feel the heat from the two bodies on either side of me. Through the window at the end of the train, I can see another group of young people dancing.

At the Sixteenth Street station, I get off and roll my bike to the exit. The escalator crowds with people, and there's a sign that explicitly states NO BIKES. I step to the stairs and look up at what appears to be about a million steps to the top. I can't even see the end. I stand there. I know which way I'm supposed to go, but I don't care. I desire the quickest, easiest way out. I hoist the bike on my shoulder and ride the escalator into the darkening evening.

Who Doesn't Like Bubbles?

I'VE HOOKED UP with Leila and Terrance this week. I feel slutty and proud, yet I'm anxious—because I'm having feelings, the surprisingly happy kind. Which makes me nervous—because I'm sure it can't last, that bad shit is about to spring up.

And sure enough—last night, Terrance basically broke up with me.

I've loved our dates. He set clear boundaries for himself, and I accepted them, because they worked for me as well. I appreciated, perhaps even needed, him to take the lead, to dictate parameters and play. I could consent and obey or shake my head no, and he'd offer another choice.

But after our talk last night—all this anxiousness—I feel like a teenager. Masturbate a couple times together and shit gets complicated.

On our third hangout a couple weeks ago, after a delicious salad that included walnuts and apple slices, he pulled me to the couch, stood in front of me, and calmly stated that he'd love to get comfy and put on some porn and watch each other jack off.

He said, Does that work for you? You know, nothing serious. Just a good time, he added for clarity's sake, I'm sure.

He shifted his weight, and I relished the movement of his hips. He waited.

Sounds adolescent but fun, I said.

Just you wait. Check this out, he said.

That's when Terrance brought out this package of jack-off toys for men: silicone eggs. At first, I was like *What the fuck,* but he's turned me into a believer: a little lube, and this stretchy silicone ball became magic. A mouth, an ass, a hand—any orifice you can imagine. We stripped and set up the computer, and each scooted down on the couch and placed our legs on either side of the screen on the table. He has regal feet, pedicured with perfectly rounded toenails.

The porn played. He kept asking me if I liked what I saw. I picked up on the fact that he got turned on when I described it explicitly: *I like the way she's sitting on his face. I like the way he's grabbing his hair. I like the way they . . .* And after like eight minutes, we both came in surprisingly hushed and tender moans.

He shut the laptop, and we cuddled up together. I laid my head on his thighs. I could feel the way his cock got softer and softer under me until it slipped between his legs and I fell asleep.

But last night with Terrance, things got a little heavy.

We were both too tired to do anything but shower and share a black-olive-and-mushroom pizza from Arinell Pizza on Sixteenth and Valencia—not as healthy as a quinoa bowl, but sometimes you have to let loose—and we watched the last two episodes of *Luke Cage*. Then he turned to face me on the couch and informed me he was heading to LA for a few weeks for some family business. That he wasn't sure exactly when he'd return, that he's enjoyed playing with me, that he hopes we can see each other again.

I hate the term *playing*, but it did describe our intimacy: jovial, physical, easy.

I sat up and said, That's fine with me. It's for the best. I mean, what else is there to do?

Hey, I don't want to stop playing.

I hate that word.

I don't want to stop hanging out with you. I'm just being transparent. Because I like you.

He put his hand on my thigh. Not in a sexual way, but soothing, calming. It worked. But his announcement reminded me that I also had to make some decisions about where I might live when my sublet ends in a little over a month.

⁂

IT'S ALMOST NOON on a Sunday, and the morning fog is giving way to sunshine. I'm walking Terrance down Shotwell to the Sixteenth Street BART like a gentleman.

But regardless of the weather, I'm in some kind of funk.

Terrance keeps singing some stupid Morrissey song, snapping his fingers as we stroll.

I say, What's up with you and new wave? Like Morrissey.

He corrects me, Like the Smiths, in that *How dare you confuse the two* way.

He stops in the middle of the sidewalk and says, I'm just so disappointed in present-day Morrissey. But I do love his early songs: Be a boy. Be a girl. Be both.

I face him and say, I like boys and girls.

He says, I do too.

I say, I know, and touch his chest through his red-and-black flannel, picturing his yummy, hairy belly underneath.

I hear Terrance ask me, So how you feeling about our conversation last night?

We are standing at a bodega outside the BART station, in front of stacks of yams and onions and fruit on rickety green carts.

I say, You're not trying to have that conversation again right here.

He says, Sure, why not? Now that you bring it up.

I say, I didn't bring it up. But I hear myself sound a bit desperate.

I say, It's been a hard year.

Terrance says, I know I've said this before, but I am so sorry about your loss. I want you to know. I'm a friend. I'm here.

We both nod and don't say anything else for a sec.

Then he says, That's why I'm all about summer fruit.

I stare at him like I don't quite get it.

He says, Trust me, summer fruit. It's all sunshine and tartness and warmth and potential. I have an idea.

He turns from me and grabs a paper bag from the cart at the front of the store and starts filling it: peaches with white fuzz, slick orangey-red nectarines, blood-red cherries.

A person comes out and scolds him—*Don't mix, those are different prices*—while handing him another brown paper bag. Terrance disappears inside to pay and then steps back outside and says, Here, feel better. And he hands me the bags, and we both stop midmoment to watch a clown on stilts walk by us, followed by a number of other characters dressed up.

Terrance asks, What is going on?

Festival at the park down the street, a woman pushing a stroller says.

Join us, the clown shouts.

Terrance says, Wanna go to a festival and have a coffee and eat some stone fruit?

Come on, he says, and puts his arm around me, pulling me forward.

On the way, we pass the Mission Hotel, and I point out the stenciled sign we spray-painted onto the sidewalk.

Am I supposed to know what that is?

Not really, I say.

But the fact that he saw it, the fact that we are heading to the same park where I first spent time with Leila, where my summer began, this little town of ours, these streets, the way things lead back to each other, the fact that everything crisscrosses and intersects, all these events coming together, makes me want to believe in something like resolution or purpose, that what you left behind—yes, the pain and anger, but also the good things, the joy—finds a way back to you.

At the festival, we grab a bench and watch the clown on stilts who passed us earlier make massive bubbles with two wooden sticks and some rope. There are community information stalls and a face-painting station and parents chasing their kids wiling out on the small grassy area. Community information stalls and a face-painting station. Someone reads a storybook about collaboration to mostly adults holding sleeping babies, because the kids are going crazy with the paletero in his beat-up straw hat. He rings his bell and jokes with all of them, and hearing him switch from English to Spanish cracks me open.

Terrance says, Huge bubbles are rad.

And I can't disagree.

Terrance stares at the bubbles and all the kids jumping up to try and pop them. I have to admit the clown has skills, because the bubbles hover over them just out of arm's reach. Like they're taunting them. Daring them.

Terrance turns to me. He says, Look at you, smiling like a fool. You like bubbles too?

He says it in this shocked kind of way.

I say, Who doesn't like bubbles?

I say it in Terrance's patented *Don't be stupid* kind of way.

He looks around and says, That woman right there. She's not even appreciating the bubble beauty that's around her.

I laugh.

He hugs me and says, You have a great smile.

I say, Are you going to tell me to smile more?

He shakes his head no and says, I stopped telling people to smile a long time ago. Instead, I thank them for their smiles they choose to show me.

I say, You're welcome.

I say, You know I just realized we've never had a drink together. I've never seen you drunk.

And hopefully you never will. I'm much more interesting this way, he says, and he ta-das like he's just ended some dance number.

He says, You know there's only one way for this all to end.

I say, You buying me a peach paleta?

He says, No. Popping bubbles.

He kisses me and lets me go and sprints up to the group of kids still jumping, trying to pop a bubble. He pops one, and all the kids stop and stare at him. He motions to one kid, and I watch him pick her up, this little child whose face is painted with glittery purple wings, and he hoists her high, and I'm worried for a second because, you know, parents.

But then she pops this massive translucent bubble.

And all the kids scream in celebration, shouting, Me next. Me next. Me next!

What Name Did You Choose?

RIGHT THERE ON the bench, watching Terrance pick up child after child, I feel such a rush of contradictory emotions: frustration that he'd just informed me he was leaving for a while, joy at the children laughing and screaming and living, and a sadness, a longing. But I know my discomfort is not really about any of that. Not about Terrance, anyway. Not about kids in a park popping bubbles. It's about painting a child's bedroom, and unwrapped baby shower gifts shoved in a storage locker. It's about me and Luna.

It all happened so fast. I'm not even sure what the word is for when you lose a child before it's born. I know the abbreviation for the medical event is IUFD—intrauterine fetal demise.

I teased Luna as she ballooned out that she constantly placed her hands on her belly like she was framing it, showing it off. She was. She always called me over excitedly to feel the baby kick right as it stopped kicking. I knew she was teasing me, waiting for the last few seconds when she knew the baby was about to stop.

She'd say, Sorry you missed it. You need to up your papa game.

So I would randomly and without notice spring up on her and place my hands on her belly to catch a kick. I'd poke and prod and cajole: *Come on, little lovebug, kick for me.* I did it this one morning and she said, Keep your hands there. I did and waited. Nothing but that hard, taut firmness I had come to love draping my arm over as we slept.

She said, I'm going to the doctor's today. I haven't really felt the baby move this morning.

When was the last time?

Yesterday morning.

Did you call them?

I'm just going to go in.

So when, in the middle of second period, the school secretary stepped into my classroom, I knew something was wrong.

She had gone to her doctor, who sent her straight to the hospital for an ultrasound, where the head nurse had instructed her to call her partner. Then when I arrived, there were meetings and consultations, everyone speaking in that serious soft tone: stillbirth, inducing labor, caretaking box, birth plan considerations, autopsy choices, informing family, designating responsibilities. I went home to grab the quilt Luna wanted to bring the baby home in and an outfit to wear and the box of Depends. When I pulled out of the driveway, I had a moment: *Turn right to head to the hospital, turn left to run away.*

I could feel disbelief course through my body. I wanted tears. Instead, I felt anger and shame and nausea, and then breaking through it all: relief. I hadn't realized how nervous and stressed-out I'd been, how I *was* worried about my papa game, that I wasn't ready. So maybe, I thought, this was a good thing. I clenched my jaw and turned right.

I did my job. I fulfilled my responsibilities. I walked up to our hospital room, far away from the other births happening on the floor, a large paper orangey-brown maple leaf affixed to the door, the signal to nurses of what was happening inside. I remember actually thinking, *What a clever way to symbolize an ending, with a marker of autumn, of winter coming.*

I held her hand. I whispered the euphemisms—*you're doing great, you're so strong, you're almost there*—over and over while they gave her a sedative, then the epidural. I left out any encouraging phrase that included the word *baby.* The nurse, an elderly woman named Jodi, guided both of us the whole time, showing me how to behave, how to act, never looking at the birth, always looking right at Luna. I mirrored everything Jodi did: I held Luna's hand and stroked her head, told her *You're doing it, you're fine* until she slept.

When she finally delivered the baby, the doctor, a handsome, regal-looking man, wrapped the body quickly and stepped to the corner of the room. I wondered if he was specifically assigned to us because of his demeanor. Then he approached me and whispered: *Would you like to hold your child?* I walked out of the room.

When I returned, Luna sat holding the baby. Jodi had an arm around Luna's shoulders, sitting next to her on the bed. Although the baby's face was covered, Luna held the hand, small and delicate, but I just couldn't. I went back out to the family room and watched TV calmly until Jodi and the social worker found me, explaining that they would care for the body for a few days in case I changed my mind about holding it. After that, they would provide us a memory box, which they give to the partner to share with the birth parent when it feels appropriate. I never shared it with Luna.

I hustled home before Luna was released. Her parents had come to stay with her in the hospital after I called and told them what had happened. Carefully, I gathered and moved every box and gift bag from the baby shower a week earlier—all disturbingly pink and blue, with crinkly tissue paper jutting out—to the hall closet, out of sight.

I stood in the baby's room: the freshly painted walls, the crib, the bookshelf I'd bolted into the wall—the last thing we did to prepare the house for its arrival. The mobile with black-and-white shapes, good for brain development, we'd read in one of the baby books, still lay on the dresser. I was supposed to hang it, but I'd never gotten around to it.

I remember searching for a screwdriver to hang the mobile. I remember that every single one I found was a standard head and I needed a Phillips. When I discovered one in a drawer in the bathroom, I didn't even try to sink the screw into a stud. I just went straight into the drywall on the ceiling above the crib. I imagined how the baby might have looked up and cooed. I sat there dreading the moment Luna would come home and all of this would be real.

☙

LUNA MOVED OUT a month after we lost the baby, which is a very typical result from that kind of trauma. I researched the statistics: the percentage of couples that split after a newborn death is staggering. At first, the anger and grieving united us, but with nowhere to direct it, what were we to do with it? One morning, she was thirty-two weeks pregnant. A week later, the nurse and social worker presented me with a memory box for our dead baby.

There is something about grief that holds on to you. Or maybe it's you holding on to it. Like itching a scab, like stroking a scar. A reminder. And nothing can prepare you for when the onslaught of grief arrives. And nothing can free you from its presence. My wife was brave enough to accept what she needed to do. She couldn't grieve while being with me, living with me, eating with me, sleeping next to me. I'm not angry, really. I understand. She packed everything up one Monday and left.

I stayed in the apartment until Metal Matt came to get me, knocking on my door one evening without warning. He stood at the threshold of the entry and waited for me to say something.

Although we talked regularly, I hadn't seen him in person for a few years. I knew why he was here. I knew Luna must have told him I was alone, that our lease was up at the end of May, as well as my teaching contract, which I couldn't bring myself to renew.

You drive here? I asked.

All the way.

You hate driving.

That's why you're driving all the way back.

I'm not ready to leave.

Who ever is? But you've got till the end of May, my friend. And I'm here to help you come home.

I shrugged.

He said, But you gotta take me to the rock-and-roll museum before we leave.

You mean MoPOP, and you've got to be kidding.

Dude, it's like my Disneyland: you know you're gonna hate it, but every music lover has to go at least once.

We packed by day. We experimented with locally brewed IPAs in the evenings in the barren apartment, surrounded by boxes and bottles, acting like we were beer sommeliers. I told him I planned to quit drinking when we got to the Bay, to have a sober summer. Metal Matt listened, never asked any questions, so I dumped everything out.

I even told him about the last time I talked to my father: as I was explaining what had happened to the baby and what had happened to Luna and me, he put the phone down and walked away, shouting obscenities in Spanish.

I told Metal Matt I just sat there for almost ten minutes before my father returned.

You still there? he said like he was shocked.

I said, I wanted to make sure you were okay.

He said, I'm fine. I walked to my front yard and yelled at my neighbor. But he's an asshole, so it doesn't matter.

I said, I understand.

But he got all serious. He said, Efren—and he never called me Efren.

He said, Listen, son, I can't do anything. No one can. But let me tell you this: Do what you have to do to deal with it, yell at your fucking neighbor for no reason, but don't become a drunk or an addict. That shit will only kill you and kill their memory. I've seen it too many times.

For the first time, Metal Matt responded to one of my stories about the loss.

He said, I know you and your pops got issues—really, who doesn't?—but, to be honest, I'd listen to that bit of fatherly wisdom.

I nodded.

Metal Matt said, It's always shocking how people can surprise you.

We rented Lime bikes, pedaling through the stunning spring sunsets of the Pacific Northwest, going to bars and donut shops and the ghosts of Seattle's music scene: the Crocodile, Re-Bar. One night, we stumbled upon the baseball stadium and noticed that the Mariners were playing the A's. We got bleacher seats and talked shit with Mariners fans, until things got slightly heated because they started talking about the Raiders leaving the Bay Area and Metal Matt shot back: How about them SuperSonics. Neither one of us are the biggest sports fans, but we were from the Bay and found ourselves flexing a bit.

I enjoyed the rush of masculine energy: all shoulders up, back erect—not yet completely bitter and toxic, more like a craving, something gnawing on the inside of you. But I scared myself a bit as well. That rush was coupled with a desire to exert, to lash out, to push back hard on something in front of me. I then understood my father yelling at his neighbor with no shame or regret, just trusting the need to attack or confront. I made us leave before the game ended.

⚘

ON MY LAST day, we loaded up a tiny U-Haul that we rented for the day with the final few pieces of furniture: an end table, a dining room table, matching midcentury modern dressers, which I couldn't bring myself to sell because I thought Luna might want them eventually. After that, the only things left were the baby-shower gifts. Neither Metal Matt nor I wanted to look into the boxes and bags. I left to get lunch while Metal Matt loaded them into the truck, along with unwrapped boxes of cloth diapers, a Diaper Genie, and a car seat. We drove it all to the storage locker.

I had to call Luna when the storage manager turned down my application because I was moving out of state.

He said, It's our policy. We need an in-state address on the application.

I snapped at him, Here, speak to my wife, and go ahead and ask her about all the dead baby stuff while you're at it.

Metal Matt slowly stepped between me and the speechless manager holding my phone in his hand.

Hey, buddy, how about you wait in the car, and I'll finish this up.

When he came out, Metal Matt said, It's taken care of for the year.

At the apartment for the last time, I walked through, taking in the kitchen, the bedroom, the bathroom, but I avoided the spare room, the one we had set up for the baby. Metal Matt stood there and waited. Finally, I made it to the door and pushed it open: that warm daffodil yellow on one wall, antique white everywhere else. Completely bare except for the mobile I hung the day Luna came back from the hospital and the crib: white and made up with fancy olive-green linen crib sheets.

Metal Matt said, You want that?

I walked up to the mobile and tapped a few of the shapes, and it bobbed and rotated in a calm, slow motion. I watched until it stopped moving.

❧

OUR LAST STOP: MoPOP.

At the museum, I loved the ephemera: the notes on napkins, the handwritten setlists, the shirts worn by band members— what I would give to smell one. One of the exhibits was centered on the toll addiction had taken on the local music community. In one corner of the exhibit, a series of photos flowed across the wall: people passed out in hotel rooms, in bathrooms, backstage at concerts. In the middle, there was one picture with a mother and father sleeping in bed, a child crawling over them in what looked to be a squatted apartment. I couldn't stop staring at it.

Metal Matt found me and stood with me.

You good?

No. I want to understand why literally just over ten months ago, I was talking with my wife about baby names and now here I am about to leave everything I expected behind.

What name did you choose?

We didn't.

The World Is a Beautiful Place

I'M FEELING SUCH relief: I acquired a house-sitting gig near Guerneville starting in September. Sadly, the drive is an hour and a half from the Bay Area, but it's free and secure for the next few months. This provides more time to find the right place—whether in the city or the East Bay or I guess even up there—to ease into it, rather than commit to something out of desperation, always a good idea. But I'm nervous that when I leave the city, I'll lose the connections I've made or reestablished with my friends, though they all assure me that won't happen. Terrance, already in LA, told me to call him anytime. Leila has been nothing but supportive about my relocation to the North Coast, saying she loves day trips to the Russian River, which snakes through Sonoma County, slowly making its way to the Pacific.

A plus: getting back to nature. I'm eager to return to the

world of plants, the rhizomes and roots buried underground, the fiddleheads and fronds. And that's just ferns, of course. Give me all the plants: the mosses and lichens, the redwoods and the oaks.

Until then, I plan to savor my final few weeks in the city and make the most of the end of summer.

Working in the corporate sponsorship department for MOMA, not only do I get free entry to the museum, but I get a discount at the coffee shop and café. Strolling the art's a plus. My favorite room is the photography room and the Jim Goldberg prints. He told his subjects to write little snippets about themselves or their life to go with their photo. His images of poor people in the city, all black-and-white and moody, their stories, in scribbly handwriting, of such loneliness and heartache—they break my heart. Sounds trite, I know, like *really*, but the photos of rich people, with their much more legible handwriting, felt vacuous, like all the stereotypes about rich people were true.

Although I'm still seeing Leila, I set up dates on Tinder. Like this one with a guy named Devon. He and his wife desire a three-way. I text him to meet me at the Richard Serra sculpture on the bottom floor of the museum.

This whole online dating game is new but disconcerting. I'm shy at first, but I can get going. I know this. I tell myself I like to be in control, meaning I really just want to feel safe. I mean, who doesn't, right?

Initially, Devon wanted to meet at a bar. I thought about acquiescing even though I'm not drinking. But I figured if I was gonna get naked and vulnerable with someone, let alone a couple, I wanted to meet out in the ugly real world, midday, no pretty lighting, no background music.

After he texts me that he's here and I tell him to go into the Serra sculpture, I walk down the wide cream-colored wood steps to the massive oxidized-metal sculpture a floor below. I feel on display. I feel eyes watching me. I feel like everyone knows what I hope to find in the recesses of steel and shadow. At the entrance to *Sequence*, the sign reads PLEASE DON'T TOUCH, but like every child and half of the adult patrons, I ignore it and place my fingers on the grainy, cold steel. Then I walk in to meet my date.

Nothing happens with Devon except for some low-key flirting in public as middle schoolers play hide-and-seek around us, but I'm still satisfied.

After work, I bike through the city to the beach by myself. My Bianchi has twenty-one gears, but I can only ever use seven of them because the gear shift is busted and so the chain is stuck on the biggest ring. It makes it so damn hard to pedal around with all these hills. I do it anyway. That pain and sweat, such a perfect remedy for desire.

I arrive at Ocean Beach, sweaty and sucking air, just in time for the last hour of sunlight. I put away my phone and earbuds. Something about the beach at dusk makes me want to listen to the world.

People stroll along the shore. A few people jog. *Show-offs,* I think—with their neon shoes and their spandex shorts flaunting sexy asses. I watch this young father and daughter—she looks to be about five—hustle across the grayish sand to the shoreline. When they're a few feet from me, the girl begins to scream for her dad to come back and take her sandals off. Like she doesn't want wet sand on her shoes, but she's cool with dry sand. I guess I get it.

But then she freaks out and starts rolling in the sand, whipping around. The tantrum is so intense I almost can't believe it's real. Sand flies all over me.

Her father runs up and says sorry, and I feel nervous because, you know, fathers. But then he kneels down next to her. I watch him slowly take off her sandals and brush off her chubby little-kid feet. Softly. Delicately.

I hear the child doing that huffing you do after you totally just lost your shit and you're calming yourself down. He sits next to her and takes his shoes and socks off, and it's strangely intimate to watch. I look away to the sunset: vibrant oranges and yellows, subtle purple on the edges.

When I look back, I see them lying on their backs in the sand, legs raised, feet next to each other. They both have bright-red painted toenails. They wiggle their toes and swing their legs and laugh.

I bike home believing the world is a beautiful place. I bike thinking of Luna and Metal Matt texting about me on my birthday, thinking of Terrance, his soft, round, warm body in that velour robe of his, the belt hanging down by his sides so that his cock and thighs peek through the opening in the front, offering me bowls of healthy food, offering to feed me. I even think of my father, his quick and sharp voice through the phone, the way he listens and then instructs—not always what I want, but I can tell he's trying and that means something.

At a stoplight on Eighteenth and South Van Ness, I'm breathing heavy, earbuds blaring some Fiona Apple song, and I'm wondering if Apple is her real name and what Spotify playlist the song is on when a car bangs into the back of my bike.

I'm pitched to the left, and the sharp pop of the bike tire's inner tube rings in my ears as I land in the street. I close my eyes and hear the faraway sound of Fiona crooning about being a criminal.

A concerned customer from the Whiz Burger on the corner rushes to me, asking, Did you hit your head?

I consider my body: no head contusion, no bone jutting from any limb, no asphalt pebbles freckling my skin. I realize I'm fine.

My bike is a mess, though, and one earbud has broken open like a small chicken egg. I stare at the damage for a moment.

The concerned customer helps me up, and I stare into the front windshield of the most beautiful lowrider I have ever seen: a '70s Chevy Nova, the hood airbrushed in browns and golds with an Aztec warrior, adorned with a feather headdress and wielding an axe. The rest of the car is candy-apple red.

The driver emerges slowly from the car, wearing a 49ers jersey, and he must be barely fourteen, and he's so nervous it makes me want to console him.

He says, How's the bumper? My dad's gonna fucking kill me.

I hear the customer talking to the driver: What about him? the customer says, gesturing at me. Do you even have a license?

The teenager leans against the car delicately. Then, like he's had an epiphany, he shoves his hand into his khakis and offers me folded bills.

I reach out and take the money. As I pick up my bike, I hear myself saying, Just leave.

He doesn't hesitate. He ducks back into the car and roars away.

I hear the customer ask, How much did he give you?

I unfold the bills and count forty-seven dollars.

I look up and say, Enough.

What Are Friends For?

WE'RE AT BENDER'S: Kay and Mike and Metal Matt and Leila and an assorted group of people on a warm Monday night. All we talk about is our collective disbelief that Nazis—like what fucking decade is this?—have been burning torches and holding rallies across the country this past weekend.

Kay says, I don't think we should call them Nazis.

What should we call them? I ask.

Kay says, We need to call them what they are: American white males.

And right then, a guy who passes as American and as white and as male saunters onto the back patio, the embodiment of bad timing. But Kay welcomes him into the small space by offering him a seat.

He says, I agree. I was telling a friend about this picture of a young white supremacist holding a torch, screaming. The caption said: *And most of these white men go home to wives and mothers who support them.*

Kay says, That's so gross and accurate on so many levels. I don't know which part is more problematic. White supremacy isn't just propagated by Nazis or Proud Boys. It's white women calling cops on Black and Brown people; it's privileges around schools and food accessibility.

Everyone listens. Kay impresses. She has a confidence and clarity with her words. Her delivery is precise, and her ability to make people feel welcome and at ease is genuine. Kay's white. Mike's 100 percent immigrant Mexican, he likes to brag. He once pointed out that I'm what their love child would look like. I said: You wish, Daddy.

Kay explains that we need to get creative in the fight against white supremacy, to imagine a future without it. I fidget, uncomfortable in my body. The phrase *get creative* makes me nervous. Like I'm choosing denial, ignoring what's in front of me. But I also realize I do really want to imagine a different future for me and for the world. I want a future where I still grieve my child and my marriage and my life but I'm able to envision a new one. Just like I want to live in a world where we remember the past but do something about changing its legacy.

Mike says, Like what the Black Panthers did in Sacramento.

Kay says, Imagine being there when they came up with the idea to walk fully armed into the state capitol. That probably sounded crazy before they actually did it.

Metal Matt says, I loved what ACT UP did at that church in New York in the late '80s, and on that TV station.

Kay chants, Fight AIDS, not Arabs.

The new guy says, I'm inspired by those Black football players who kneel during the anthem.

Leila says, But really it shouldn't be Marshawn or Kaepernick. It should be all the white players.

I stare at her like *Who the hell is this football-watching person?*

Kay says, Perhaps that's the real question. What do white people need to do to stop white people?

No one says a thing.

When Leila and I leave, we walk to her place. It's quiet along Twenty-Fourth Street. We don't really say much. We enter her apartment, then her room. She dims the lights and kicks off her shoes. I do the same. She puts on a record. It's an old one. The yellowed paper sleeve falls to the floor. It's some type of jazz, a bit discordant but not jarring. I say, Who is this?

She faces me.

She says, The divine Melba Liston.

We close our eyes and listen.

She says, Can we just hold each other tonight?

I say, I'd like that.

She says, There's so much wrong in the world right now.

I say, You're right.

But my response sounds stupid, so underwhelming.

I say, I lost a child recently. A baby, actually.

She pulls away to look at my face. I realize I don't really know how to tell the story of it—of loss and trauma—not sure of the right distance to keep.

I say, It's fine.

But I know I'm lying. And I am no longer interested in lying.

I say, It's not fine, but I'm learning how to be okay with it.

I was trying to say that I completely agree with you about the world, but I now appreciate all these little things that I never really considered important before, that I realize are the most beautiful parts of the world.

Like what? Leila asks.

Like tonight. Like political discussion with friends and strangers at bars. Like learning about new music. Like cuddling.

She chortles. I realize I don't want anything else but this moment. Not a beverage. Nothing physical. I'm content.

She begins to pull off her T-shirt, but she gets her head caught, and after a second of struggle she laughs because she's stuck.

I say, Wait. Don't move.

I stare at her.

I say, There is something so beautiful about you.

She says, With my shirt over my face? Fuck off.

I say, No. Not that.

I reach out and stroke her chest, rising up and down with her breathing, her biceps, her armpits, slightly moist, her underarm hair splayed out, wild and dark.

I say, Let me help you.

I do, and the shirt slips from her body, and she looks at me and says, Thank you.

I say, What are friends for?

The Strange Reverence for Our Bodies and All Their Messiness

IT'S THE END of August, and my sublet expires on the thirty-first, but I can stay till the end of the weekend. Instead of a goodbye party, this is my farewell spin class. I made everyone I care about promise to come today. I've been attending the studio regularly all summer. It's a queer-owned spin studio with bikes set up in a circle and only one fan. So the room boils, but it's got a great sound system.

After class, we all plan on heading to the counterprotest to the Nazi gathering scheduled downtown. But come tomorrow, I'm busing up north to Guerneville.

All five of us—Leila, Kay, Mike, Metal Matt, and me—meet at the corner coffee shop forty-five minutes before spin class. That's nine fifteen in the morning on a Saturday. No one's in a good mood except Leila, who sports puffy-butt bike shorts in a shade of yellow that might be illegal it's so bright. She munches an almond croissant.

Everyone else grips their coffee cups like they need help balancing.

Me and Metal Matt both wear black basketball shorts and grimy white tank tops.

Kay says, Did you two coordinate?

Metal Matt says, Style just comes natural to both of us.

He hugs me.

I kiss him on the cheek.

Mike says, I hope your ass don't break during the class. Mine always does, and that's why me and Kay came prepared.

They both turn their asses to us and pat them like they're proud. They, too, are wearing puffy-butt shorts, thankfully in more muted colors than Leila's.

Kay says, It's not really the ass, though. It's the taint.

Leila says, The perineum, if you want to get technical.

I watch her mouth move, covered with fine white powder from the croissant. She grins. Metal Matt and I look at each other. I'm not sure how to feel about everyone reflecting on the health of my taint. So I laugh.

I say, I actually have been having some issues. I mean, every now and then. Hemorrhoids anyone?

Kay pushes me, saying, TMI, Chino. Damn.

Mike lets loose his chuckle that makes it look like he's getting punched in the gut.

Metal Matt changes the subject saying, Will the pain prevent me from protesting Nazis today?

Leila says, How quickly do you heal?

Metal Matt says, Hmm, never really hurt my taint before.

Kay says, I just want to acknowledge this moment as the best morning conversation ever.

I step away to get some water while they discuss the requisite dexterity necessary for icing a taint.

I asked Stevie, the spin instructor, to make an extra-special musical playlist for my friends.

Stevie is one of those instructors who loves that she's mic'd up, urging us *Faster* and *Harder* and *Turn that tension dial a quarter more.* She wears wild leopard-print pants with these almost obscene see-through mesh patches that ride her muscular thighs. Her top is covered by a pair of neon workout shirts and a headband holding back her short, curly hair. I love headbands, some deep fetish coming from highlights of lithe men playing tennis, with names like porn stars: Björn Borg and Andre Agassi.

There's about twenty of us ready for class. Usually, I hide as far from Stevie as possible, because I'm lazy like that. Today, she makes me ride next to her, and so I make Metal Matt sit next to me and so on down the line: Leila, Kay, Mike.

Stevie comes up to Metal Matt and says, I like all that hair. You want a scrunchie?

Mike says, He sure does, and I bet he wants a butt pad.

Stevie, still staring at Metal Matt, says, Don't we all want that, honey, don't we all.

The mic syncs to the sound system with a beep, the lights dim, and she says, Morning, everybody. This is a goodbye class for Chino, who's been sober all summer. In times like these, it's the little things we need to celebrate. So today: Chino.

She claps and makes everybody clap along as a song by the Red Hot Chili Peppers comes on: *I like pleasure spiked with pain . . .*

Stevie yells, Let's warm those legs. Today's playlist is full of '90s power ballads to work that body and prep our souls to confront those Nazis. Can I get a thumbs-up?

I'm already huffing, my body relaxing into the motion, giving in, while all the people around me, a circle of mostly women, raise their thumbs.

Stevie shouts, Can I get a Fuck Nazis?

We all shout, Fuck Nazis.

Stevie says, That's a trick question. If you can talk, you're not working hard enough. So get ready, my beautiful people, let's spin.

The power-ballad melodies continue on our faux outdoor bike ride: Linkin Park's "Numb" for our first climb; Bikini Kill and Hole for our sprints; Faith No More's "Epic," L7's "Can I Run," and 4 Non Blondes' "Spaceman" for rolling hills. For our long, slow mountain ride I requested specifically Metallica's "Enter Sandman." Metal Matt smiles at me as the first notes ring from the sound system, his loose hair bun bobbing.

For the finale, Stevie turns off the lights. She walks the circle, pats each person's handlebars, and says, Let's go deep. Let's close our eyes. Let's turn that tension dial as far as it goes and then take off one turn. So this hurts. This should be painful but, most importantly, doable. You can do this. Repeat after me. *I can do this.*

We all, in various forms of distress, shout: *I can do this. I can do this.* I have a moment of panic, recalling the darkness of the room in the hospital with Luna, the smell—visceral and sharp and metallic—the strange reverence for our bodies and all their messiness. I remember telling Luna she could do it, over and over, and feel the anxiety creep up in my chest. I focus on the present: the smell of old sweat in the room, the huff of my breathing. I tell myself: *This is for me.* I shout a bit louder: *I can. I can. I can.*

Then, like some perfectly timed bad video, the slow opening sounds of Staind's "It's Been Awhile" pulses through the room. It has to be the best worst song ever. I can't help it. I feel all emotional or spent or in need of a hug. The singer sings lines about not being an addict and not being alone. I bike hard to hold it all in. I bike like I can outrun everything or like perhaps I can catch up to something.

The class ends, and Stevie hugs me. She shakes hands with all my friends and says she hopes they come back. She stops in front of Metal Matt and says, How's that ass?

Metal Matt releases his hair and says, I'll let you know.

I swear Metal Matt blushes. Me and Leila wide-eye each other.

Leila steps close to me and whispers, Need me to check yours?

I want to answer, but everyone is around me, sweaty and flushed and waiting.

When we step outside, the counterprotest has found us. Like something instinctual, we all check our phones and discover the Nazis no-showed at their rally point at the Embarcadero, and rumors are swirling that they're hiding in some cheap motel. Instead of waiting, the counterprotest morphed into a street party: a row of clowns playing horns; parents pushing strollers; kids running in the streets; union groups with banners full of acronyms, chanting; people shouting through bullhorns alongside antifa waving black-and-red flags, with literally the entire group in faded black clothes, their faces covered by dark cloth. The whole spectacle is inspiring: beautiful and ragged and incongruous. Cops march along the sidewalks. They strut by us, and like another instinctual compulsion, Metal Matt and I flip them off. They smile and salute back to us. I feel conflicted.

Leila says, I planned this. I brought the party here to you.

Kay and Mike hug me. They kiss my cheeks, and Mike says, Come back any time. You know you got homies here.

Kay says, You do. Be safe.

They run into the street party.

Metal Matt says, I'm gonna go fuck with some fascists. Call me when you get settled.

We hug, and I feel the wetness of his shirt. I say, You look ridiculous, and you're all sweaty.

He says, I feel ridiculous.

He smiles and leans in and says, But my taint does hurt like hell. And you should tell your doctor about your butt. Check that colon.

He pats my ass and walks away. Then I see the paletero. Or, rather, I hear him, even over all the other racket. I'd know that bell anywhere, its rhythm and sound: *da-ding, da-ding.* I grab Leila's hand, and we rush over. He's actually wearing a black handkerchief around his face like he's ready to join the street battle. His eyes glint. His cart covered in cartoonlike stickers for ice cream. He has a handwritten cardboard sign that says: PALE-TAS FOR EVERYBODY $1, PALETAS FOR NAZIS $1,000.

Leila says, I love your sign.

He says, I made it special for today, but really it's for every day. It should be like this every day.

He makes a sweeping motion with his arms.

I say, It really should be like this every day.

He gives us a thumbs-up.

I realize I have no cash and look at Leila.

She takes out a five-dollar bill and straightens it, nice and crisp, and hands it to him.

Leila says, Keep the change. I'll have a fresa. And she looks at me.

I say, I'll have a coco.

The paletero rings his bell and moves on down the street. People flow by us. I savor the cold coco. I watch Leila suck on her fresa. I have this urge to make some wild, joyous noise or to hop up and down or to race through the crowd.

Leila says, I loved the class. Thank you for making that happen.

We stare at each other, the chaos streaming by, and continue slurping our ice creams.

She pushes me and says in the best spin class instructor voice, You can do it. You can do it.

I smile. We bang paletas, and drips fly onto each other's hands. We both lick them off.

She says, How about you write me a postcard when you get settled and invite me up for a river date?

She grips my free hand and taps her paleta against the back of it. Looking in my eyes, she pulls my hand to her mouth and licks the dollop of ice cream off my skin.

She gives me a thumbs-up and turns, and I watch her step off the sidewalk, walk a few feet into the crowd, and spin back to look at me, raising her arms like we'd won something, like whatever comes will be faced, like we *can* do it. Then she's swallowed up by people, by the joy of the march.

I lose sight of her, but no matter.

I know she's there.

What Some Things Will Do to Survive

IT'S MY LAST morning in the sublet, and I'm in the tiny kitchen, making myself a sandwich and cutting it up into manageable pieces to eat with a fork, because I love basic PB&Js but I hate the stickiness of jelly as it oozes out the sides. It makes my fingers tacky, films up my phone screen, and if I bite the sandwich as a whole, I can taste the sweetness on my lips at random moments for hours afterward.

I stare at the perfect square, and I recall how Luna used to tease me that I'd mess up our kid's childhood with my weird and deep-seated PB&J issues. Let the jelly spread and ooze, she'd say, and I explained that if I kept an even margin on each side of the bread, when placed together, the delicious insides could spread but not spill over.

I think about my mom and her bananas. When I was a kid, I envied my friends whose parents bought multiple boxes of cereal—I had a multitude of choices whenever I spent the night at someone else's house. At home with Mom, I'd wake each morning to a note saying why she had to leave the house early and a bunch of bananas purchased from the dollar bin. One night when I was about twelve, I complained to her that I hated them, black-spotted and smushy. My mom tried to convince me that those were the tastiest spots, that the flavor of the softness was superior, but I knew better. They were cheap. They were spoiled, rotten. The next morning, I rose to find a bowl of bananas cut up with the bruised areas removed. But I threw them away, desiring a bowl of Cap'n Crunch and a new mother.

Maybe it was a good thing that Luna and I didn't become parents. Kids can be awful.

I place the sandwich cubes in a warped piece of Tupperware with a suspect lid that keeps wanting to pop off. I try like ten times to make it fit to no avail when I realize I might miss my bus, the 101 express from San Francisco to Santa Rosa on Seventh and Market. I call an Uber and grab my duffel bag, packed with everything I own.

I forgot to pee before I left, so I'm all anxious because the trip's two hours with no traffic, and what are the chances there's no traffic? With minutes until the bus arrives, I hustle my way into the Carl's Jr. across the street to find a bathroom. The place is tore up: people look like they're camping at some of the tables: bedrolls, Ikea bags bungeed at the top, hiking backpacks. I don't even stress about the sign announcing RESTROOM FOR CUSTOMERS ONLY and sprint to the back, but a woman stands ahead of me in line. I keep looking at the bus stop and shuffling my feet.

The door opens and the woman says, You in a rush?

I nod. She motions me in.

I say, Thank you so much.

She says, Just call me the Good Samaritan of bathrooms.

After, I rush back right as the bus pulls up, like a boss.

I choose a seat near the back with space all around me. This young guy gets on wearing a muscle shirt and smelling of flowery cologne, the sides of his head shaved and his flattop all spiky and gelled. He sits directly across the aisle from me, and I'm like *Homie, why?* but I don't say anything.

Not ten minutes later, he asks to use my phone to call his ride waiting for him. I hand my phone over, and when the lock screen disappears, my Tinder app pops up, still open.

He cackles when he sees it and says, Dude, swipe right on everything. It ups your odds.

After he calls his friend, I feel him watching me as the bus bumps and chugs in the Sunday afternoon traffic, people returning to their suburban homes from a weekend in the city. An hour into the ride, as I fork bites of my sandwich into my mouth, I glimpse him chewing his nails, leaning against the window, stealing looks at me like he wants to talk.

I turn to him and say, Want some?

He says, Never turn down food. That's what my pops always taught me.

I say, My father taught me the names of wildflowers and bushes in New Mexico. That's about it.

Damn. You still know about plants?

Mostly.

What's that?

He points out the window at the wide brown fields somewhere north of San Rafael. In the middle of them are scattered oaks, massive and old, branches twisting and bending and beautiful.

Those are oak trees. There used to be thousands of them all over this area.

I hand him the warped Tupperware, with visible blobs of jelly and chunky peanut butter stuck to the insides. He doesn't hesitate, quickly grabbing one square and placing it atop another. The jelly touches his skin. He tosses both into his mouth and grins, like he and I are on the same team.

He gives the Tupperware back to me and licks each finger on both hands loudly.

He says, Thank you, my man, and kicks his feet up on the armrests of the chair in front. He closes his eyes and softly hums a tune. It's strangely familiar and intimate, his voice baritone and soothing. He's got on Timberlands, with the laces all loose and tucked into the shoes, rather than tied. Soon, he sleeps, and it's so peaceful. I watch him for a while before I turn back to my window and the farmlands racing by.

The times I went to visit my dad in Albuquerque, he always took me on his errands, driving around the city to houses full of friends and acquaintances. I'd wait quietly next to him as he caught up with everyone, never really paying much attention to me. But then we'd head out beyond the city limits, to the mesas and arroyos and mountains to the east. It was then he'd tell me the stories of various places, how Indians settled here or fought off whites on that mesa. He'd point out plants, tell me their names—names which later I learned weren't correct, were just what he and his friends had called them as kids: arbolito, oído, agudo.

When we reach Santa Rosa, the guy high-fives me as he struts down the aisle, excited to be getting off the bus. I'm continuing on to Monte Rio, but as we enter Guerneville, about four miles before my stop, the driver says, Journey ends here, folks.

None of the four other single male passengers complain that the *journey* was supposed to end ten miles up the road, over in Jenner. I don't want to be that guy because, you know. I give the driver a dirty look and bound off holding my duffel.

It's hard to stay mad on a day like this in Northern California, a late summer afternoon, a Sunday, when you've got nowhere really to be.

But now I have to piss again. I meander into town and see an older lady out in her front yard in full gardening mode, surrounded by piles of cut hydrangea flowers and green leafy tree branches.

I say, Do you know where a public toilet might be?

She points with her shears and says, To the end of the road and make a left at the light, and there are some public bathrooms at the beach park.

I hustle down River Road into Guerneville, with its empty storefronts next to high-end restaurants and wine shops. I pass a huge, boarded-up old movie theater with a whole campsite set up in the closed-off entryway. Just down the street, I peer in the window of a fancy German restaurant called Brat, with a cute queer couple sitting in the window, eating a fancy hot dog with a fork.

Up ahead, I see the beach park and a building that must be the bathrooms, and I start to hustle there.

Yo, man, the bathroom's locked, a voice shouts at me on my left.

You're kidding me, I respond, and look at the two guys

lounging in the shade of a tree, sitting on their own backpacks. I realize I don't know which one spoke to me. We stare at each other.

The guy on the right, sporting a bandana around his neck and this shit-eating grin, says, Why would we kid you?

He turns to his friend with hair cropped close to his head, and says, He thinks we're kidding him.

The other guy says, I heard that. He looks at me and says, Why do you think we'd kid you? We're trying to help you.

I say, Help me by telling me where I can piss without having to buy something.

They both stand in unison, and one says, Follow us.

The shorter one grabs a half-full box of Tecates. They march down the sidewalk ahead of me. It really is gorgeous: an elegant line of redwoods in the distance, a green, green canopy of trees. The day is warm, with a breeze that teases and cools you every few minutes before the afternoon falls back to stillness and heat.

The guy with the bandana struts—confident, entitled— grimy and grizzled in the sunlight. I'm a bit on guard.

He says, without looking back, I'm Shawn with an *h* and this is Buddy with a *B*.

Buddy with a *B* shoves Shawn with an *h* in this tender way.

We come into sight of the Russian River, flowing evenly and incessantly, glinting in the sun.

I say, I'm Chino.

They stop in front of a liquor store.

Shawn yells from the open front door, Hey, Hunter, can this guy use the toilet?

Hunter, a tall man in a black beanie, with a superskinny face, says, It's all stopped up, man.

The two turn to me, and Shawn says, You shit out of luck.

Buddy giggles and shoves a can of beer in his friend's hand and then my hand, and he shouts to Hunter, You hear that? *Shit out of luck.*

Hunter responds, That shit is funny, man.

This makes all three toss their heads back and laugh, wide-mouthed and genuine, full of something like faith and bravado.

I chuckle once. I feel my laugh build. I let it fall out of me. Gain speed. Join the others.

I say after a minute, Luckily, I don't got to shit. I just have to piss.

Shawn says, Come with us, Chino.

I follow them off the sidewalk and across a field littered with blackberry brambles and tufts of mean and yellowed grass. We come up to a grove of eucalyptus trees, the tops of which sway in the breeze. We get to the edge of the bank, just above the river, and we can see the path descending to the beach below. I take in swimmers and a colorful array of beach umbrellas. The guys crack their beers and chug. I hold mine. I haven't had a sip in over two months.

I open my can and watch the white foam bubble over the top and down my fingers, dribbling to the ground. I sip it, and it doesn't taste anything other than exactly how I remembered it tasting. I'm not sure how to feel about the familiarity, the bodily memory.

We stand and stare out onto the easy flow of the river. It's peaceful. Divine, even. I think of the bus driver saying *Journey ends here.* I think of the final four miles I have to go to Monte Rio and how I'm going to get there.

Buddy with a *B* then throws his can to the side into a clump of bushes and unzips his pants, keeping his belt buckled.

Shawn follows. His can floats and glints across the air.

I'm stunned. I haven't seen someone litter so boldly, so cavalierly, in forever.

I can't muster the courage to chug beer, so I toss it to the side. It thuds on the ground and a puddle of white foam pools around it on the dry dirt trail. I unzip and watch the arc of my piss unfurl into the air.

As we meander back toward the main road, a snake suns itself in the middle of the path. We all stop and watch it. No rush. Only fascination. It's rich-brown-and-cream-colored, with dots of sharp yellow, and has the most perfect geometrical design running along its body.

Buddy says, That's just a gopher snake. I used to love holding snakes as a kid. My dad would catch 'em. He was such a prick. You know how dads are.

Both Shawn and I mumble in agreement, which makes me look into each of their faces like we've connected or something, like we are children of fathers, and we definitely know how they are.

Buddy says, He loved snakes, though. He had a pet python he'd let us hold.

Shawn says, What happened to it?

Buddy says, It's the only thing he took when he left my mother.

We both *mm-hmm*, because what else?

I say, I was like five or six, and my father and I were camping in New Mexico, and he called me over, all excited like he'd found some treasure. He opened his hand, and it was a lizard. I remember it had these little horns and beady eyes. He told me to grab it by the tail. So I did, and he let the lizard go, and it swung for a second in my hand, and then the body fell to the ground, and I held this wiggling tail in my fingers. I freaked out and started bawling.

They laugh like it's the funniest thing they've heard. Even more than me being *shit out of luck*. What can I do but laugh as well?

Shawn says, That's so fucked.

Buddy says, What did he say?

I say, First, he told me I killed it, but when I freaked out even more, he told me to relax, to stop crying. He said the lizard was fine, and then—and I remember this so clearly—he said, Isn't it crazy what some things will do to survive?

Now no one says anything. We just stare at the snake. It feels a little awkward.

Buddy then tries to grab it, whispering, Here, snakey, here, snakey, but it slithers quickly away.

We enter the town and head west to get to its edge. On the outskirts, I drop my duffel bag, and Buddy offers me another can.

I say, I'm good.

You gonna try to hitch?

Either that or walk. It's not too far.

True, but be careful on the highway in the dark.

Thanks, I say.

Buddy with a *B* shakes his head like he understands, then turns back. Shawn with an *H* does the same. They both say, like they do this all the time, Fare thee well.

I watch them walk away and listen to them still talking about the snake. I enjoy their easy friendship. They stroll away like kings, down the sidewalk leading back into Guerneville. I realize that they probably left knowing better than me that three dudes trying to hitch a ride was a lost cause.

So like that, I stand alone on the side of River Road at the western edge of Guerneville.

A bus like the one I got off a few hours earlier rolls on by, passengers visible through the windows on their way to the coast. I shake my head like *Unfuckingbelievable*. I watch cars accelerate as they leave Guerneville proper and pass me by without slowing. Finally, I raise my hand and put out my thumb. I'm a hitchhiking virgin. I realize all the stuff I know about hitching is romanticized. Two hours go by, and the light begins to darken and fade. I realize I may never get a ride, but here I am.

I've gotten this far, and I've got time.

I can walk it if I need to.

I can make it there.

I know I can.

PART TWO

Life Cycle of a Fern

Fall 2018–Winter 2019

From *Ferns of Northern California*

Ferns, whose habitat is the moist, shaded rocks in redwood forest openings, are common along the Pacific coast. With their versatile absorption habits and their deep network of roots, they can withstand cold, drought, and flame. The most successful ferns are limited to tropical habitats, where they have become treelike, extending forty feet or more into the air. When they come to life each spring, they have shiny, dark stripes on their broad, triangular fronds, which possess a waxy powder that can rub off to make a print.

Chino Learns about Fire

Do you want to see a match burn twice? my father asked me one day. We were sitting on the couch. We were alone, which, for me as a child, was a rare occasion. Knowing my father, I was certain it was a trap, but I said okay anyway. I craved the attention. He took out his matchbook, something he always had on him. Sliding it from the pack of Kools, he struck a match, and it sizzled into a flame. He let it burn. A match burning is a beautiful thing, like a fist unfurling. I watched, waiting. He looked at me and then back at the burning match. I listened to him inhale and blow it out. Then without hesitating, he touched the ember, orange and glowing to my forearm. *Get it?* He laughed. *It burned twice.* Despite my shock, my pain, I didn't cry out, even as I flinched away from him. I remember thinking he'd be disappointed if I did. It's a trick that will only work once. I often wonder how long he waited to play it on me. I marvel at his patience, his determination, every time I touch the scar.

Chino Remembers Being a Child

The puppy's neck snaps so easily I don't even realize I broke it. When my mother comes to check on why I'm crying, she yells *Move* and pushes me out of the way. It's not often my mother hits me. Her hand on my face sounds like what I imagine a broken neck would: high-pitched and acute, sudden and final, a branch breaking, a door slamming shut. I tell my mother that I was just trying to move the littlest puppy to the nipple. I tell my mother the bigger puppies kept pushing the little one off. I tell my mother the little puppy kept turning its head away from the nipple, so I tried to turn it back. I only wanted to help. Later, when my mother comes to say good night, she doesn't say sorry. She says that the puppy would have died anyway. That it was the runt. That sometimes there is nothing you can do. Sometimes helping only hurts. She rubs my back for a minute. I feel small and delicate under her hand. When my mother leaves, she turns the light off and closes the door. It doesn't make a sound.

AFTER MY MONTHLONG house-sitting gig ended, I rented a cozy cabin shrouded by redwoods, smack in the middle of the Russian River Valley. There's a smattering of oddly quaint communities—Forestville, Rio Nido, Monte Rio, Jenner, and others. My cabin sits in a small cluster of homes all built in the early 1900s outside Guerneville, south of the river. Once the skies cleared every morning, that sharp blue autumn sky astounded, the fresh air, the scent of decaying and wet things.

I walk frequently through the fire trails and the long-established pathways that meander from one community of houses to the next, sometimes skirting abandoned off-the-grid cabins, old mills, an occasional plot of marijuana, then suddenly dropping into the end of paved street leading back to the one-lane road that connects everything on the south side of the river.

But mostly, it's just me and a stunning variety of mushrooms and ferns.

The only shitty thing is that one-lane road following the river. It twists and bends in ways that make it so you can't anticipate oncoming cars at all. You have to drive basically five miles an' hour as you approach each turn. It's enough to have made me reuse old coffee grinds, because the thought of driving it was too much.

When I moved in, I purchased a white-and-yellow '96 Ford Ranger that belonged to a pest extermination business. The first day of my lease, my old-man neighbor, Mr. Garofalo, warned me to take it easy driving. He said to make a list before going and check it before returning, because there's no turning around on the river road. He added, Don't be ashamed to ask a neighbor who's headed toward town to pick something up that you forgot. We've all done it. It's called a river-road grovel.

He's been living here forever, and he's more than willing to educate me on how things work. In retrospect, he proffered this advice and then asked if I had any beer he could have because he was out. I gave him a couple Tecates, because he seemed like the kind of old man who when you asked to borrow a socket wrench would ask: What size socket you need?

He encouraged me to make a grab-and-go bag in preparation for a speedy fire evacuation. He then informed me that usually by the time we were told to evacuate, it was too late to drive out on the road and, in fact, driving was discouraged to provide room for emergency vehicles.

Then how do we evacuate? I asked.

The river, he said, with a tone that implied it was a stupid question.

But added, Unless the emergency is the river flooding. Then we're good. We're above the flood zone. Just hope you have enough water and food for a week or so. That's why your shopping list is crucial.

He was also excited to inform me that he knew one other Hispanic who lived in the area.

❧

WINTER PASSED, RAINY and monotonous. Spring, though, is something else. The money Luna and I had put aside to allow each of us to take a full six months off to parent our child was quickly running out. I began to feel a bit anxious about ever finding a job that would both pay me a decent salary and satisfy my desire to show children the outdoors. And, of course, this disdain for any other kind of work made me feel all privileged and shitty. I refreshed Craigslist every couple of hours, until I saw a job with the Sonoma County Outreach and After-School Programs Division for a science tutor serving kids who live in the area.

I immediately applied and got the job, because I was the only applicant with a degree in a hard science. I didn't care. I felt elated, ecstatic. I even told Mr. Garofalo when he came to see if I had any beer he could have.

The class will be held in a community center a few miles down the road from my cabin, in a park that abuts a huge section of BLM land and numerous trails through redwoods. I would be responsible for eight children in the seventh and eighth grades, and I was warned to be very careful because there are four boys and three girls and one *they*. The supervisor, Mr. Rogers—*No relation,* he always adds when introducing himself—whispered this under his breath like it was something dangerous.

When I meet all the kids, I can't tell what gender half of them are, all in pants and shirts, some with short hair, some long, with names like Forest and Lyric. There's one kid named Bobby who could pass for every Bobby bro I've ever known, but regardless.

I introduce myself, I'm Chino Flores. You can call me Flores. Anyone know what that means in Spanish?

Floor, the kid named Forest shouts, not even looking up at me.

I can't tell if he's trying to be funny or really thinks that's what it means.

I'm sensitive to this, because during my entire first year of high school everyone called me Kentucky. It was my first day, and I was trying to impress my new classmates in third-period geography by being the first to respond when the teacher asked for states that began with the letter *C*.

I shouted, Kentucky—and never lived it down.

I say, The word for "floor" is *piso* in Spanish. Flores means "flower." So call me Mr. Flores or Mr. Flower. And today I'm using he/him pronouns. Let's introduce ourselves to one another.

No other child gives their pronouns except one: Forest. They.

Problem solved. I feel slightly clever and effective in my role as teacher until Bobby screams at me to come over: Mr. Floor, Mr. Floor, check this out, all these bad words written on my desk.

Mr. Rogers encourages us to get outside but suggests we avoid the trails on the hill behind us, because the area burned this past fire season. But it's wonderful to walk those trails—warm sun, not too hot, no more trace of the smoky air—so I decide: Why not take them there?

All along the path, mushrooms jut up everywhere. As we walk, the kids chat a bit, joking mostly about magic mushrooms vs. poisonous mushrooms, but since it's uphill, everyone's also focused on breathing.

When we get to the fire line, we stand in silence, because the landscape stuns: the smell sharp, reeking of smoke, the tree trunks charred, portions all cindered and brittle, the forest floor strangely mottled, black ash and brown earth.

But the most amazing thing: in the midst of all that destruction are thousands of mushrooms and tiny green things, a "fire bloom," scientists call it. All these fronds and petals and the tips of branches are sprouting everywhere—maybe snowbrush, *Ceanothus velutinus*, and white spiraea, *Spiraea betulifolia*, and checkermallow, *Iliamna rivularis*.

Nobody says or does a thing until Bobby and Forest start clapping.

I'm not sure why, but we all join in.

I will spend the rest of the spring and summer hiking this trail with these children.

I will never cease to be amazed by how the forest rejuvenates, how it heals.

From *Ferns of Northern California*

Ferns and mosses are some of the first greenery we see after a fire. They have rhizomes, horizontal stems tucked away underground that stay protected and help them survive the extreme environmental events they must endure.

IN EARLY NOVEMBER, the fires return, and we are told to leave immediately. I step out the front door to see a slowly moving police car crawl through the windy streets, blaring: *Please evacuate the area, road open for evacuation until 9 p.m.*, on repeat. I see Mr. Garofalo holding his grab-and-go bag. He waves at me and says, Can I catch a ride? Without waiting for a response, he tells me to grab my bag, along with a couple beers for the road. I don't hesitate. He opens one before I even pull away.

We drive along back roads, the sky all apocalyptic, dark and smoky, to his buddy's house in Santa Rosa. He complains about either my driving or the state of the world the entire way. When we arrive, his buddy hugs Mr. Garofalo and pats him on the back, guiding him into the squat '50s-style house's front porch. It's tender and casual, and I wave at him, and he waves back. I have nowhere to go, and since there is no set date to return to our cabins, I head to the Bay, to my friends.

Metal Matt welcomes me into his apartment, wearing an orange sweatsuit. Record crates line the entryway, so I roll my evacuation bag—a pink thrift-store-purchased piece of luggage packed with a couple days' worth of clothes, extra charging cables, an off-the-shelf toiletry kit, my important-papers lock-box, and two books—to the corner of the living room.

I sit in the chair across from him on the couch. He hands me an N95 mask.

I say, You're actually going to wear that out in public?

He says, Have you seen the sky?

I say, I think that I've actually tasted the sky it's so smoky up north. I just drove through miles of it.

He says, It's not like we're going to wear them forever. Just a week or so.

I say, I'm beginning to think every fall will be fire and mask season.

Metal Matt stares at me for a second, like he's sussing something out, like he's waiting for me to break.

And he always wins.

I say, Luna texted me to see how I was doing, said the anniversary is coming up in a couple months. Like I don't know when the anniversary is.

I use air quotes to indicate that *anniversary* is a fucked-up word to describe the death of our child.

Metal Matt crosses his arms and nods, but he remains silent as I let my feelings course through me.

Someone knocks, and Metal Matt acts demure: Who can that be?

Kay and Mike stroll in: Kay, in overalls, and Mike, in blue Dickies and his white shirt. They both declare it an SFSU reunion. Metal Matt pours us each a glass of sparkling fruit-and-tea combo, his new nonalcoholic beverage of choice.

Kay says, So Metal Matt tells us you've acquired a new job.

I say, I have. I found this perfect job teaching after-school science, but basically we hike most afternoons in the redwoods or along the Russian River.

I tell the story of Bobby and how he still calls me Mr. Floor and I can't tell if he's destined to be a bully or a comedian.

Is there a difference, really? Mike asks.

Humor, Metal Matt responds, like *Obviously*.

I tell them about Forest and their pronouns, and Kay shares that preferred pronouns are a thing now, even in elementary school.

I admit to them, These classes do make me think about starting a program like this on my own, something that isn't just prioritizing the state curriculum's science goals. I mean, we live in one of the most diverse bioregions in the world. I've got the credentials. Just gotta figure out a business name.

Metal Matt says, You've sold me, Bill Gates. You sound hella inspired.

I jump to my bag and unzip it to grab my computer. Out falls one of the books.

Mike picks it up.

You've had this book since college?

Since before, I say. It was a gift from my father to my mother.

Mike opens it and reads the handwritten inscription on the cover page of *Flowers of the Southwest Mountains* by Leslie Arnberger:

Violet, some of these will be popping up when you return from the Orient. Hope we can enjoy them together.
Elias

They never did. I know this because my mother, Violet, returned from "the Orient" to Santa Fe, the city of my birth, but not really to my father, Elias. She'd had other plans.

Mike says, It's kinda creepy reading intimate notes from one parent to another, am I right?

Metal Matt says, Better than just watching them fight all the time.

We all stare at him, because we know exactly what he means.

I say, It's the only thing left I have of hers.

Kay says, I'd argue that you may not have a lot of material things left from her, but we all have a whole bunch of emotional and psychological shit—or should I say gifts—from our childhood.

Mike says with a perfectly straight face: I think I'd rather have the material gifts. Because really, how does any child survive childhood?

Kay Tells This Story about Her Childhood and *The NeverEnding Story*

There is a line in the movie *The NeverEnding Story* that made me a writer, showed me how language can mean so many different things at once. This character, Rock Biter, says, *They look like such big, good, strong hands*— after not being able to keep his friends from falling into the Nothing. He couldn't protect them. No matter how strong you are, you're not strong enough. I look at my hands now, strong and capable, and I remind myself to hold on but never to squeeze. I remind myself to touch all my friends while I can.

Chino Tells This Story about His Mother

My mother never wore a bra. Instead, she regularly wore T-shirts with phrases like FLAT IS BEAUTIFUL or BOOBIES ARE FOR BABIES, her little breasts hanging low, her nipples arrogant, hard, always poking through the material. It embarrassed me. When I was fifteen, I asked her as she was getting dressed, *Why, Mom? Why don't you even own a bra?* She turned to me, shirtless, and asked, *Do you know the reason men have nipples? No,* I said, and shrugged. She said, *To remind them of what they could have been.*

Metal Matt Tells This Story about His Stepfather

When I was ten, I hated my mom's boyfriend. He hadn't earned my anger but there wasn't anything he could do to avoid it: My two brothers and I had just been uprooted by divorce and forced to spend the summer with relatives who pitied us. Our mother moved to southern Oregon ahead of us, and when we finally were reunited with her, she was living with him: this chubby white dude from the East Coast who refused to let us touch his things, drink his soda, or cuddle in bed with our mother. One night, he called me to the living room. He was in his chair, listening to his music. He shrugged and said, Your mom wants me to spend some time with you. I know you don't like me, but you might like this. He handed me an album. He showed me how to place a needle on record. *Master of Reality* by Sabbath begins with a cough and ends in a void. Thirty-four minutes and twenty-nine seconds. I wish I could get that first moment back. Like the first kiss, like the first time on ecstasy, shit will never be the same or as good. He said after, I'm not the best with words, but listen to my music anytime you want, and maybe we can be cool with each other.

Mike Tells This Story about His Best Friend, Garrett

It's impossible to feel your own uvula without other distracting sensations: your fingers on your chin, your jaw opening wide, the stretch of your tongue. So my friend and I decided to touch each other's uvula, that moist red protrusion we all grossed out on. We were thirteen, and looking for any reason to touch other people's bodies. So imagine Garrett on his knees, my finger elongated, my other hand resting on his forehead, I reached in, trying to avoid the walls of his throat, and suddenly felt it: surprisingly firm, erect, warm. Garrett looked at me, eyes wide, as vomit erupted from his mouth. He slowly got up and went home. We never spoke about it again, but I still remember the warmth of his mouth.

From *Ferns of Northern California*

Ferns can lie dormant for many seasons, sometimes for more than a decade, without sprouting or blooming or propagating. They adhere to rocks or exposed tree roots or trunks or even other plants. They enter a period of stasis not unlike a chrysalis; then, when the situation is safe or healthy—scientists aren't quite sure exactly what triggers the process—they simply bloom.

I FINALLY FEEL at home here, a part of the rhythm and flow of how life works, after six months of living in my cabin. Like today: I hiked in the redwoods, found a tick crawling up my leg before it bit into me, swam in the river, and received a postcard from Kay and Mike wishing me a happy birthday and announcing their engagement. I talked with Metal Matt for a while on the phone, who told me about the new non-tech-centered collective workspace in Fruitvale he's joined part-time to help him with his side hustle: selling records. He spent a lot of time telling me about his new friend Suzi, the organizer/founder, who's super into spreadsheets and cryptocurrency. Metal Matt found the place through a Craigslist ad. Since he was the first one to join, he was able to claim a large closet for his record crates, which, since I've known him, have traditionally dominated each of his apartments over the years.

The way Metal Matt shared all these details, it was so obvious.

I said, First off, what the hell is cryptocurrency? And why are you telling me about her like that?

He said, Like what?

Like you're nervous for me to meet her.

Homie, I'm not nervous for you to meet anyone. But be

careful—she will definitely try to educate you on what crypto is if you give her the chance.

Let me guess. You bought some cryptocurrency and—

And what?

I refused to say anything, just waited him out, and, for once, I won:

Fine. Yes, she's refined and successful.

And . . .

And attractive. Also thoughtful. But we're just friends.

And the sound in his voice, the eagerness, the excitement, filled my heart with this strange sense of possibility, of potential.

Before it gets dark, I head out to pick up groceries (I had my list down by this point) and a six-pack to drink on the riverbed later, under the nighttime sky that, when it's clear, shocks in its arrogance and glory. Everything that gets me down just falls away under something that confident.

It's an early spring afternoon, the heat and chill mingling in the air. The smell of redwoods is sharp and rich.

I come face-to-face with this driver, and they stop and idle. My Ranger is on the outside of the curve with nowhere to go, no spot to pull off. I can't even reverse out of the bend. I wait, because they have room to scoot over so I can squeeze by.

The driver raises their hands like *What do we do?* I wave them to the side and begin to inch forward. We each proceed slowly, haltingly, until we crawl past each other with seriously like an inch to spare on each end.

When we get across from each other, I see that it's a woman with a cigarette in her mouth. She rolls down her window. I lean out mine, ready to snap *It's called being considerate,* but she interrupts: Listen, sweetie, I've had a couple Manhattans.

And pauses.

Like that explains everything: how we got here and where we're going.

She then smiles and shrugs.

I stop speaking and—I can't help it—I smile back.

How do you respond to that? Being called *sweetie*, I loved it.

I say, No worries. Take your time.

She says, That's all anyone can really do. But I've seen your truck a few times. You living here?

Yes, on Redwood Drive, next door to Mr. Garofalo.

Lucky you.

He's a bit—

Of a pain in the ass.

I was going to say nosey, but yes.

She says, Welcome. And maybe I'll see you around.

She then inches forward but keeps looking right at me.

I wave my hand, motioning her on like I'm a gentleman.

Then she stops and beeps.

I lean out and crane my neck to look back.

I see her silhouette. She doesn't try to turn around but says, And, sweetie, if you can, grab me some cheddar cheese and tortillas.

Is this a river-road grovel? I say, feeling some strange sense of belonging.

You call it what you want. I call it a friendly favor. Just leave it all in the mailbox at Oak and River. I'll find it.

It's pitch-black when I start driving home. This time, I don't encounter another car. My truck squeaks up to the mailbox. I step out, and the evening sky sparkles and preens above me. I can't hear the river, but I know it's there, flowing and bending and finding its way out to the ocean. As I place the tortillas and a bag of shredded cheddar cheese in the mailbox, the thought of a warm quesadilla delights me.

I dump the apples out of the compostable green plastic bag. Hoping it doesn't tear, I drop a handful of cheese and two tortillas in it. I take out my list and write, on the back of it, my name and number.

I add, so it doesn't seem weird: *A friendly favor from your neighbor.*

I have to scratch out my first attempt at *neighbor* because I spelled it wrong. But whatever. That's not really the point, is it?

I write: *It looked delicious, so I borrowed some. Thank you.*

And a smiley face. I also included a beer from one of the two twelve-packs I went ahead and bought, knowing Mr. Garofalo would ask me for one at some point in the next few days.

Anyway, I don't think she'd be offended that I took some, and I don't really care if she calls. But standing under that sky, thinking of some warm food and a beverage, it felt nice to know she might. Even just to say thank you.

SHE CALLS A week later.

She says, I'm Genevieve.

The way she says her name riles me: all elegant and multisyllabic. She says she's heading out and asks if I need anything. The way she says *need*, or maybe the way I hear the word *need* and consider all the possibilities, the way she is so matter-of-fact, like she wants absolutely nothing from me, makes me realize I am hungry for something her voice reminds me of.

Lately, Terrance has been sending me sweet, random pics whenever he thinks of me: a persimmon or a fern—especially ferns, to test me to see if I know what kind it is. He also texts me pictures of secret little spots that would be perfect to hook up in. Mostly bathrooms. I sometimes reach out to Leila too, who's met someone else and moved down to San Jose. I'm happy for her.

My instinct is to protect myself, so I say, No I don't need anything at all.

Definitive. Unwavering. I'm proud of myself.

She says, Okay, and without hesitation, she ends the conversation.

I may not know what I need, but I know I'm not being honest.

I call back in about five minutes and say, Yes.

She waits.

I say, Can I ride with you?

She asks, If you know what you want, just tell me.

I laugh.

She waits, though, not letting me off the hook. It's an awkward silence. At least for me, because I know I'm thinking about anything other than items at the grocery store. And I have no idea what she's thinking.

She says, Meet me at my mailbox in thirty minutes, and disconnects.

It's been a cold winter and spring, but it's beginning to get warm, the magnolia trees in bloom, the plum trees raining down their white-and-pink petals, the baby neon-green tips of the redwoods. I admit to myself: I feel fertile amid all this new growth.

I dress in freshly washed denim jeans and one of my few button-down shirts, vintage Montgomery Ward, with a printed triangle pattern. I examine myself in the mirror, consider how I might look to someone else. I know what's going on. I feel it all in my body: I want to be consumed. I want to be enveloped and overwhelmed and safe. I don't want to be rigid or shut off. I want to let go and be caught.

I'm not sure why I sensed something with Genevieve, but I'm trusting myself.

We drive in silence. I watch her take up the whole one-lane road, and when we come upon another driver, she idles there waiting for them to adjust to her, even when it's easier for her to adjust to the other driver. I'm appalled and aroused. She has her hair, a grayish-blond color, pulled back tightly, wears blue jeans, boots, and a flannel jacket. She carries herself with an air of authority and nonchalance.

We stop for a cocktail at the Forestville Club. I've never been there. Three men sit next to each other at the bar. Across the room, there's a huge parquet dance floor surrounded by some beat-up chairs and tables. On the tables are ashtrays with actual butts in them, something I haven't seen inside a bar in forever.

We haven't talked much, just made casual conversation.

She tells me to get her a Manhattan and whatever I want. She then takes out a cigarette and lights up.

It's four in the afternoon on a Saturday, so what else am I going to do?

I get two Manhattans.

I place them on the table. She immediately extinguishes her cigarette, slides the bright-red maraschino cherry off her toothpick, and pops it in her mouth. As she chews, she reaches over, takes the toothpick from my drink, and places it in her own.

She says, I don't need any drama. Especially where I live.

I nod, back straight, eager to hear her out.

She says, I get the sense you are available.

She waits.

I realize I need to affirm yes or no.

You mean, am I seeing anyone else?

I don't care about who you see. In fact, I would prefer that you do. I care about: if I start seeing you, will you cause me problems when we stop?

You mean, will I stop getting you things from the store if you need them? I joke, trying to act relaxed.

She says, I like things clear and concise. I'm fifty-eight, and I know what I want. I've been married a few times. I have grown kids and grandkids. I've got enough money coming in that I can do what I want. I have a lover in Santa Rosa. But you're a bit more convenient.

I chuckle at that and raise my eyebrows.

I say, Thanks, I think.

She says, Sorry. And cute.

She reaches out and pats my hand.

She says, So if you can handle it, we can have a good time now and then.

I nod my head but think about kids. Think that if things hadn't fallen apart, I'd never have met Genevieve. I wouldn't be on a stool at the Forestville Club. But I am here. This is where I am.

I say, Thank you for your clarity. I, too, like the convenience— and the energy you give off.

I move to take a sip of my Manhattan, but she says, Wait.

I say, I find you attractive and compelling . . .

She says, Stop talking. Turn to me.

I do.

Pick up your drink.

I do.

Sip it slowly. But look at me as you do it.

I do, and the cold, slightly viscous liquid, sharp and sweet, enters my mouth. I hold it there and look into her eyes and wait.

She says, You can swallow.

I do, and she leans back in her chair holding her cocktail glass with both hands.

I like to watch, she says.

I say, You can watch me do anything, lowering my voice, like I mean something secret— dangerous, even.

Her eyes go deeper, darker. She picks up the toothpick and slides the cherry off it and says, You'd be surprised at what watching reveals.

I nod in agreement, but really I'm staring at the way her mouth moves, nibbling on my cherry.

She says, So tell me, what do you want?

Chino Reflects on Genevieve's Question about His Desires

It's awkward to ask to be bitten—hard. The sensation of teeth on a forearm, teeth on the back of the neck, the inner thigh, the calf, beautiful teeth leaving such glorious bruises: it exposes some primal desire to be enveloped and loved, the way a mother dog picks up her puppy by the scruff and places it down safely. *Bite me,* you say, meaning *Love me,* meaning *Hold me,* meaning *Take me home.*

Chino Considers Where Desire Comes From

When my mother splurged, purchasing ripe raspberries from the store, she'd dole them out two at a time like rewards, little payoffs. When she left the house, I'd steal ten, lock the bathroom door, slip one after the other onto the tip of each finger, like ceremony, like foreplay. I'd revel in the delicate balance between expansion and destruction, between pushing too far or not far enough. I felt dirty and unclean. I felt excited. In the mirror, I'd deliberately tease my own mouth, ask quietly: *Do I deserve this divine reward?* I'd say yes but think no. I'd feed myself the berries one at a time, whispering to my reflection, flush with desire, that I was such a good, good child.

I HEAR MR. Garofalo yelling, so I know Kay and Mike must've parked in the wrong spot, which according to Mr. Garofalo is any spot he doesn't approve of. I hurry out the door and intervene, reassuring Mr. Garofalo that they're with me, that I invited them here, that they're not—in his descriptive words—tweaker trash from Guerneville.

He has a point, though. Lately, a few vehicles have appeared in the mornings, parked along River Road at various turnoff points, with belongings stacked in the passenger seat and people sleeping in the back. I ignore them. Mr. Garofalo, on the other hand, has no patience, and he basically escorts them out of the area. And there're some shady folk milling outside the one Safeway in town, mostly white, definitely suspect. They usually drive some pretty beat-up cars, which is why Mr. Garofalo yelled.

Mike says, You calling my car a bucket?

We all turn to stare at Mike's light-blue 2010 Subaru Outback, purchased for the bargain price of $1,000. It's got over two hundred thousand miles on the odometer, but it's incredibly reliable, he insists.

Okay, I see your point, he admits. He laughs, and I realize I've missed his presence, the guttural sound he makes sharing his joy.

Kay and Mike are up here looking at venues for their commitment ceremony, their tentative description for getting married, the celebration to happen a year from now: spring of 2020.

Kay enters my house holding, in one hand, this small collection of books held together by a length of jute and, in the other, three miniature bottles of champagne. I know it's called jute because that was what Luna and I used to wrap up little flower bouquets at our baby shower.

I say, I see from the jute and the sample champagne—or should I say: sample-pagne—that you're awash in sample wedding material.

Mike says, I need the sample-pagne now, because, ugh, all this is all so overwhelming.

Kay tells me, We want to avoid the word *wedding*. How's *love celebration*?

Mike grimaces and says, Hmm, how about—dramatic pause—*celebration of desire*.

No one says a thing. We all just sit in a confused moment of reflection.

Kay looks at Mike and says, like she's exhausted by it all, Does it really matter what word we use to describe it?

Mike says, What did you and Luna call it?

Kay looks quickly at Mike.

But I say, It's okay.

I say, I'm okay.

I say, Luna and I called it our *honeywedding*.

I remember how she coined the phrase: We had been dating for three years and were on a romantic summer road trip through the Southwest after our first year of teaching. We'd agreed to not visit any family. However, as we entered New Mexico, I caved.

I hadn't seen my father in a few years, so I let Luna convince me to reach out as we passed through Albuquerque, the city he'd moved to when I was a teenager.

He met us for dinner, and he and Luna took to each other immediately. I sat there as he went on about the geological history of New Mexico, about the water crisis facing the Southwest, about how Las Vegas, Nevada, should be stopped.

Luna chuckled and said she agreed, but she asked, *How do you stop a city?* and my pops answered in this quiet tone, as if he were revealing the secret of all things, *You stop the idea behind a city.* And he tapped his head like everything made sense. When we left, my father pulled me aside and said, *If you ever have a chance to marry that one, do it.*

As Luna and I drove away from Albuquerque, I told her what my father had said to me.

She was quiet for a minute, then abruptly pulled off the freeway onto a deserted exit ramp. A glowing Chevron gas station sign emitted the only visible light as she walked around our Toyota Corolla. She opened the passenger door and pulled me out, and took me to the front of the car and told me to cover my eyes.

I did, and when she told me to open them again, I saw she had written in the fine layer of desert dust on the hood of the car, *Here's your chance: Marry me?*

I burst out laughing. *Right here?* I said.

But the way she looked at me—like it was a moment for me to prove something to her, to show my faith in her—I fell silent. I felt uncomfortable in my body. She looked so calm, so grounded. So I said, *Close your eyes,* and she did, and I wrote on the hood, hot from hours of driving, *YES!*

I said, *Open up*, and pointed to the hood.

She placed her hands on my shoulders and kissed me.

I smiled and said, *Where will you take me for our honeymoon?*

Luna said, *Right here. Right where we are. This is it. This is our honeywedding.*

We made it official at Springs Preserve, right outside Las Vegas, two days later, surrounded by blooming desert agave and cottontop cactus.

Kay claps at the story and passes out the little bottles of champagne, and we each undo the tops, three little pops. We all emit little shrieks as the sparkling wine overflows, and we each try to drink it up before it spills.

Kay hands me the little pile of books. The top book is called *Ferns of Northern California.*

Kay says, I found them at this lovely used bookstore in Santa Rosa, and I thought of you.

Mike demands I read passages from the fern book, because I'm the only one who knows how to pronounce all the science-y shit: his words. We finish the champagne samples and move on to the cheap beer that I usually keep around for Mr. Garofalo.

I read: *This book is about ferns and fern relatives, plants that never bear seeds.*

Kay moans like that's such a terrible thing: to never bear something.

I continue: *Of these plants, true ferns have large leaves with many veins. The rest have small scales or leaves with a single vein. The most common shapes for the ferns of Northern California are: tongue-shaped, as with the* Ophioglossum—

Is there a picture of that tongue-shaped fern? Mike says, sitting up.

I pass the book to him.

He says, It totally looks like a tongue. I'll never be able to look at a tongue the same way again.

Mike juts his tongue out at Kay, and Kay says, Oh, I may have to steal that move.

I look at them, trying to figure out what they are talking about.

I say, What?

She says, I transitioned to substitute teaching because I'm going to grad school to get an MFA.

She raises her hands in victory, and I start clapping.

She says, So I started camming again to supplement my income.

Mike says, You mean to *actually make* some income.

I say nothing, because I'm not sure what she means.

She sticks out her tongue and arches her back, and I don't think I've ever noticed the way her jawline and neck flow so wonderfully into her chest. She jumps up and spins around, stopping sharply with a hand on her hips, looking fabulous and in control. She then breaks out into laughter.

She dazzles, and I understand.

Mike says to me, Continue, continue.

I return to the book:

For an adult fern to be deemed a true fern, it must possess both fertile and sterile fronds on the same body. This is a marvel to discover, evidence that the plant has gone through many life cycles to reach this maturity level or to arrive at—as scientists like to describe it—its true form.

Kay says, That is beautiful. To be so sure. To name it. To know something is true.

Chino Learns That What We Say Matters

As a child, I loved roughhousing, the chase and yowl of tag, the arrogance to face a speeding baseball and catch it without flinching, making your father proud. The crazy way dodgeball works, looking one way and slinging a purple rubber ball in another direction, anyone fair game. But one game haunts me. It was my favorite, played with a group of boys and occasionally a few girls, if we were lucky. The rules: you threw a football high into the air and whoever caught it ran away, ran for their life, laughing and screaming because every other kid tried to tackle them and usually every other kid did, a massive writhing mound of prepubescent bodies, piling on top of each other. I still recall the smell. It was the greatest. Everyone called it Smear the Queer. One day, my mother asked how I got a bloody nose and a ripped shirt. *Playing Smear the Queer,* I boasted. To this day, I remember the look on my mother's face. And the question she asked me: *Do you understand the meaning of your own words?*

Mike Learns Teasing Is Not a Form of Loving

The kid wore this Batman outfit, with this Batman doll in his hand, and he was radiant. I was waiting for the elevator at the Alameda County Courthouse to submit my teaching credentials. The adults with the kid were talking errands and visiting family members. The kid whisked his cape around his face. I said, *I love Spider-Man too.* The kid looked at me like I was an idiot. I laughed. I couldn't help it. I kept wondering where this desire in me came from: to show love through teasing, to needle for attention, to set up contention as a way to connect. One of the adults intervened: *Is that Spider-Man?* The child laughed like some wild thing. We all entered the elevator, and the adult said, *Can you push five for me?* The kid bounced like he was waiting for more numbers to push, like he'd been told he can only push the numbers people request. Without missing a beat, I asked him, *Can you push ten for me?* Even though we were on three. Even though there were only six floors. Let me tell you—the kid stopped bouncing, staring at parallel rows of numbers that ended at six, and he made this growl, something between frustration and delight. The adults glared at me. So I said real quick, *No one else is here. Just push them all.*

Kay Explains to Chino and Mike Why Calling Something True Is a Powerful Thing

I grew up with the ocean. In Lincoln, along the Oregon seashore. I knew intimately the ebb and flow of the tides, the pull of the current heading a particular direction and how to use it to get back to shore. I can still close my eyes and remember almost instinctually the moment you stand to ride a wave, that split second you let go and join its force and movement. There is an energy there, old, unstoppable, inevitable. You can feel it deep within. When I returned recently, I walked along the coastline, admiring the sea stacks, the arches, beautiful and grand. But these rock formations are also a warning, a threat, the markings of the tide going in and pulling out, over and again, relentless, unwavering, without pity or mercy. When I feel like nothing will change, I remind myself to trust my friends, who love me. And to listen to my heart, its constant rhythm. I remind myself of the soft, lulling tides that one day will shape everything they touch.

From *Ferns of Northern California*

Before scientists understood fern reproduction, it was mystifying to them, appearing as if ferns simply grew from nothing. They couldn't find any seeds or seed casings. It is true that sometimes a fern may self-fertilize. However, more commonly, ferns send spores, rather than seeds, far and wide, increasing the chance that they will land in a supportive environment and take root.

METAL MATT TURNS forty next month, and Korn is finally back in the Bay Area for the first time since its *Follow the Leader* twentieth-anniversary tour. It's too good a coincidence. The universe is clear: I have to take Metal Matt. We both have a sweet spot for the cheesy. At least that's how he explains his love of pop and mainstream music in relation to his moniker: everyone needs a little cheese in their life, a little joy.

We first met at the Fillmore at a Hole concert during college. Sweaty and glowing from the show, Courtney jumped down from the stage after the last song, the venue lights blared and popped to life, and she just strolled through the crowd, joining the throng filing out. I tracked her and was kind of floating along in her wake when someone grabbed my shoulder and said, *That's her, right?* and I'm like, *It is,* and the person kept their hand on my shoulder. We tagged along with her, past the free event posters and hippie apples being handed out, past the security guards at the exits, down the block to the bus stop for the 38 Geary, heading downtown toward the Tenderloin. That's where she stopped. We continued a few feet farther to not be creepy, but still.

I looked at the person beside me and took him in: this white dude with a shaved head and a red beard, wearing a red-and-black flannel, baggy jeans, and Vans.

I stepped away instinctively, like *I don't know you*, like *You're not my type*, like *Maybe I need to protect myself*.

The guy said, This is amazing. Is she waiting for a bus? I'm Metal Matt. Want a drag?

I didn't smoke, but it felt like the moment I should say yes, so I leaned in and pursed my lips, and the guy cackled.

Cute, he said, and placed the cigarette gently to my lips.

Courtney did, in fact, board the 38.

We stood on the curb, and the bus pulled forward, waiting for the light to change. She was sitting at a window right in front of us. We waved, and she blew a kiss, and the bus took off through the intersection.

Metal Matt and I spent the next two hours sharing everything over Jack in the Box burgers and fries, around the corner from the Fillmore: where we were from (him: born and raised in Concord; me: from various towns between here and Santa Fe), our college (we were both SFSU undergraduates; him: a sociology major but leaning toward sound engineering; me: botany, focusing on native California), our love of music, especially singing along with pop songs, and our mutual need of a roommate, but ideally a friend.

Metal Matt believes we were destiny. I believe the timing of the Korn concert is the perfect example of kismet.

I procure two tickets for the Fox Theater in downtown Oakland.

I text him: *Reserve the Sunday after your birthday for me. I got a surprise for you. We can walk your dog, get some food, and go to a show.*

He texted back: *Perfect, because I have a surprise for you too.*

I'm dressing for work when the phone dings again. I unlock the screen, expecting Metal Matt to explain his cryptic surprise.

Instead, it's a text from my father. He says he's had a heart attack but that he's fine, he's back home. He wants me to call him when I have a minute. *Call me back,* he texts three times for emphasis.

My phone buzzes. It's my father. I stare at the screen, the word *Padre.*

I decline the call.

I'm already a bit on edge and feel myself wanting to avoid talking with anyone but a friend. Even my students Bobby and Forest could tell I was grumpy after I snapped at them during class. On a normal day, I would have loved their idea of going to search for a den of otters someone's father told them about.

It's because Luna emailed me a few days earlier. We never emailed, so it felt foreign and formal and just plain awful. Like this is what we have come to:

Dear Chino,

I'm writing for a few reasons. First though . . . hi. I really really hope you're doing well. I've actually started a new teaching position this month, and it's nice to get back to work. I heard you're also doing some after-school work. You were always so good at working with people. Especially children.

It's been more than a year now. I am still so hurt and angry and sad about what happened to our child, but those feelings also apply to what happened between us. I'm working on that—on the feelings around our relationship.

Which leads to the final thing and what prompted the email: the storage locker. I got the renewal bill for the year. I'll pay it. It's not much, but that's not the point. It's something we should deal with.
    Love,
    Luna

Love, Luna. How banal, how boring.

I put down my phone, and peek outside my window at the massive trunks of the redwoods. At Mr. Garofalo, standing by my truck expectantly. He knows my schedule—that I have to leave at two to get to the community center on time. I know he must need something.

Mr. Garofalo yells, Chino, I need a jump.

I go out to meet him and start digging through my truck's toolbox for cables.

I ask, You have kids, Mr. Garofalo?

He opens the hood to his truck.

Two sons. One in LA, and one in Medford.

Talk to them often?

Not as often as I should. Things were different then. Men and kids didn't really do much together. I mean, I took care of everything. I loved them.

You miss them.

I don't really think they like me all that much. As I said, times were different. Maybe your culture does things differently.

Mr. Garofalo, you do know I was born and raised here.

Sure. I mean no offense. Maybe it's an Italian thing. Or—you know—a man thing.

He moves to his truck, and so do I.

I turn the ignition, and my engine revs to life, then his does, and I see his image through the windshield, the jumper cables connecting our trucks.

That afternoon, at work, my father calls me again. I stare at the phone, watch his name scroll across my screen again and again, until it goes silent.

I'm supposed to review worksheets related to each student's grade-level science standards, but I can't face this bureaucratic teach-to-the-test-type curriculum today. I take my eight kids outside. It's perfect weather. We meander into the redwood grove that basically contours the river. I point out the different types of mature ferns, noting the way the fiddleheads look like dragon tongues and the fronds like green butterfly wings or large monster hands.

Forest keeps trying to climb the trunk of a redwood and yelling *I want to be as big as the tree,* and I think of how I felt a similar thing: how I dreamed of being tall, big, and powerful like all the men of my family. I wanted to be the one who presided over those who were smaller, the one who chided others to pull it together when they were weak, the one who never, ever fell down. But walking with these kids under the redwoods, I feel childish, ashamed by my misguided sense of height, of what makes something tall or big or manly.

I think of Mr. Garofalo. I think of my father. Why I'm hesitant to call him back. I think of the men in my life I love: Metal Matt, Mike, Terrance. Okay, maybe I don't *love* Terrance, but I appreciate him. Maybe times are different.

I gather the kids and say, These redwoods not only are huge, but they also protect what is smaller with their canopy.

They only kind of pay attention. They know teacher voice when they hear it. But I continue regardless.

The branches way at the top, they house whole ecosystems up there, and—listen to this—even when redwoods die and fall, all these little bugs and animals and plants take root or seek shelter or find a home in their decaying bodies.

We walk to a fallen trunk, and I use a stick to peel back a piece of bark, and, sure enough, insects of all shapes and sizes scurry out.

But then Bobby says, It's just like big piles of horse poop. If you flip them over, you'll find hella nasty bugs.

Right, I say, just like a big pile of poop.

WHEN I ARRIVE at Metal Matt's apartment—dubbed the Pink Palace because the entire building is a perfect salmon exterior—for his birthday concert, he pours us a glass of his new obsession: probiotic green juice. We wear matching black Levi's and Nikes. I'm sporting my favorite yellow button-down shirt. I'm freshly shaved, lined up, and trimmed. I feel years younger than I am. Metal Matt sports a long sleeve business shirt, and there's something sexy and perverse about his billowing reddish-brown hair and beard against the crisp white button-down tucked nicely into his waistline.

Sabbath breathes heavily in the corner, exhausted from his walk to Peralta Park, up the street.

Metal Matt says, Did you hear? Kay and Mike scoped out a place in the neighborhood. But they still love their tiny-ass apartment in the city.

I say, When you have a home, it's hard to move. I've been up north for almost a year and a half, and I like it. But someday I want to move back here. Even though I love my cabin in the trees. My job with this group of kids. And other things.

I dramatically sip my probiotic green juice.

Well, that was obvious. What other things?

I've been seeing someone. It's very adult. We calendar dates. We barely text except to confirm. The few times we ran into each other in public, it was like we were strangers.

Metal Matt has this funny look on his face.

He says, And you like this?

It works. She's in her late fifties, superclear with her boundaries. Really takes charge, and I kinda need that right now.

Chino, that's fantastic. You deserve it. Have you talked with her about . . . things?

Kind of.

He stares at me.

Trust me, we really don't talk that much.

Okay, well, you kind of stole my thunder, buuut . . . Suzi and I are dating.

I knew it!

We high-five, and he says, She sounds a bit similar to . . .

Genevieve, I say.

Yes, Suzi is clear and direct, not a lot of drama. Which works for me. Listen, she even made me sign a workspace relationship form, so in a way we have a legally binding hookup agreement. You'll love her. She's coming over to take us to whatever surprise show you've got planned. Come on, tell me, it's Lana Del Rey. She's playing at the Greek.

You wish.

You know I do.

I stand up and hug him. Something about this makes me hopeful about the world. Sabbath barks at my movement and bounds up to join us, almost knocking me over. Metal Matt and I jump up and down, and by the time Suzi walks in we're watching Korn videos on YouTube in preparation.

I've been looking forward to this, she says, and drops her leather side bag on the ground and slides off her shoes

Sabbath hustles to her and sits like he's been doing this every single time she comes over.

Metal Matt pops up and steps to Suzi, who has short black hair and these aviator-type glasses. She, too, is wearing a nice button-down shirt and slacks. The two of them look really good together.

She says, So Matthew has told me all about your burgeoning interest in crypto, and I'm here to answer all your questions.

I smile and look at Metal Matt. He laughs.

I say, Well, Matthew here might be exaggerating a bit.

I figured.

She moves to the kitchen and grabs a beer as we still hold glasses of green juice.

Since Matthew has been lying, tell me a little about Guerneville. I love it up there.

I go through the generic list: great little cabin, interesting neighbors, easy job.

She says, Is that your plan, teaching?

I think I'd prefer to open my own little after-school wilderness program. I've got the credentials and education, so I can jump that hurdle. I came up with a great name: the Wilds. So it can be in any city I'm living in. Guerneville Wilds . . .

Oakland Wilds, she adds.

I point at her like *Exactly*.

She says, So teaching them about flowers and trees.

Metal Matt says, But also big things too, like the climate crisis.

I say, Of course, but I want to talk to kids without shaming or scaring them about things they want to do or have.

Suzi says, I read all the time about the ordinary, everyday things that exacerbate the climate crisis: cars, cell phones, eating meat, crypto. Even having a child. I mean, I'd like a child someday, but who would ever consciously bring one into the world without serious consideration?

The mention of having a child reminds me that Luna and I fought the first few times she mentioned going off birth control. Then one night, she stated: I stopped.

I sat for a second and said, Okay. Do you want me to buy condoms, or do you want to risk it?

She said, What is life without risk?

I wonder how I might respond now, after everything. The thought of Luna, of holding her hand, of mimicking what the nurse did to comfort her: stroking her forearm, staring into her eyes, ignoring everything that was happening around her, with her body. I remember Luna handing the body of our baby back to the doctors, wrapped up tightly in that hospital blanket edged with soft pink and blue.

Suzi leans forward and puts her beer down, her expression concerned and serious as she realizes what the topic had brought up.

Listen, Chino. I'm sorry.

Oh, no. You did nothing. I just get hit with it now and then.

She breathes out audibly, like letting something go.

I say, In fact, I didn't really want kids in the first place.

No one says a thing after I admit this.

I say, So on that note, I am trying to find a therapist. But they're so expensive.

Suzi says, Might be cheaper down here. There are so many damn therapists in the Bay it's ridiculous.

Metal Matt says, without missing a beat, Another reason to move back.

After Suzi drops us off outside the show, Metal Matt tries to take a selfie in front of the marquee that states, with no sense of irony, KORN, and then, under, SOLD OUT.

As we enter, we experience that familiar energy: the crowd thrums with eagerness, like a first date going well, that initial brush of knees under table or fingertips to forearm. People are walking around the venue, getting beers, an ocean of long hair and black shirts and so many patches. We grab a back wall section on the main floor and wait, each holding a beer. The smell of bodies distracts, slightly arousing and nauseating.

Metal Matt says, Hey, wanted to check in about that kid convo. Are you good?

I say, Actually, I wanted to check on you. How are you dealing with *Matthew*?

I kind of like it. Much better than simply Matt. She was the first one in a long time that asked what I wanted to be addressed as. And for the first time in a long time, I decided to go with something different.

I say, It works for me, Matthew.

He says, No, you, my friend, please call me Metal Matt.

And with that, the lights dim, the crowd roars, a rush of bodies surges forward and sideways, and the sounds of thousands of

138 | Tomas Moniz

people singing along to "Got the Life" and "Freak on a Leash" and a dozen other songs I didn't know. I let myself get lost in it all: the smell of excitement, not sexual but animal, the bodies bumping and jumping. The pit: So much more than violence, than aggression, all rage and anger and fuck. A solid connection to being human, being together, a prayer in action, supplication to motion, the bouncing bellies, the swinging arms, the sweaty shoulders. And when the lights come on, an exodus: Metal Matt and I and everyone else all walk out, and I'm hurt and sweaty and my ears ring because I forgot my plugs, but I feel full and alive.

Violet Flores Told This Story about Elias to Chino

The first time your father saw you, arms chubby and legs fat like little sausages, he poked at you and said, This one's a Chiconky. It was just like Elias to mash two things together into a new thing: Chicano, honky. I always loved him best when he was with you, especially when you were a baby. He'd tease you as he changed your diaper: What's the brown part of you? He'd point to your belly, That's the white part of you, for sure. He'd point to your penis, That's definitely the brown part. He was awful, but adorable at times. He'd always end by saying, But no matter—I love every part of you.

Elias Flores Told This Story about Violet to Chino

Ahhh, son. I'm sorry. The world lost a good one. Your mama was a good woman. And what I mean by that is she knew how to show you the truth through all the bullshit. Listen, she told me about grief when we first met, and I'd lost a bunch of friends. About not drinking or partying or acting out when you're in pain. That won't help. I had issues with her, but that was some real wisdom I still pass on today. Listen, I remember the first few nights after you were born, she finally let me in to spend the night, and I remember the way you cried: Not painful, not hungry. Just sort of lonely. I remember I was worried, and she told me to go speak to you. I called you by your name: *Efren Flores*, I said. *I'm here*. But you continued to cry. Your mama told me to pick you up, so I did. I picked you up. I held your little naked body against mine, took off my shirt so you could be against my skin, and this did something for you, because you fell asleep. And that was when your mama said to me: *How do you feel?* And I said, *Wonderful*, and she said, *Remember that. When you take care of something, you're really taking care of yourself.*

MY FATHER PASSED away.

I never called him back when he texted me over a month ago.

When my phone buzzed and I saw the 505 area code pop up, I figured it was my dad—he frequently acquired a different number. I declined.

A minute later, my phone buzzed again, indicating that the caller had left a voicemail.

My father never left voicemails.

Hi, Chino. It's Maggie. Your father passed on, and we're having a ceremony. Your familia would love to have you.

I listened to the message repeatedly, searching for clues to how, to when, for any info that might allow me to not call back. I reread the last texts from my father: *Call me back,* repeated three times.

I didn't want to go.

It was Metal Matt who, though unavailable to join me, encouraged me to take the trip.

He said, Listen, you loved your dad, right?

I said, He was complicated, but yes.

We are all complicated. Just go so it's over and you don't have any weird guilt around not going in the future. Plus, you never know what might happen.

Terrance—the third person I called after Metal Matt and

then Mike, who also couldn't go—agreed to join me. He struck the perfect balance of concern and possibility around the trip. In the days leading up to our departure, as we coordinated his flight from LA and mine from Oakland, he texted that we could play if I wanted, but he explained he's been seeing someone special, someone named Marco, and although they're not exclusive yet, it was serious. I assured him that it would be fine. A formality, really. That I just needed a friend.

It's a brisk November night when we meet up at the car rental agency in Albuquerque, the sky wildly clear in that southwestern way: black sky, large blue moon, stars upon stars reaching toward the flat horizon. Terrance looks good, dressed in this wild knockoff Gucci sweat suit. His head is freshly buzzed, and he looks darker than usual, like he's been in the sun.

Don't I look saucy? he says as he saunters up to me.

I say, Delicious. LA's been treating you well.

He pulls me to him, hugging me hard at first, like he means it, then soft, and I feel his belly relax against mine as he exhales. I smell his sweat and travel and something earthy.

I rent a car to drive to Las Vegas, New Mexico, an hour and a half up the highway, but not just any car. The rental place accidentally ran out of the economy-size car I reserved, so they are happily upgrading me to a red convertible Mustang. When you open the doors, a galloping horse appears illuminated on the ground. I make Terrance watch me open and close the doors over and over, make him lie down on the ground with me taking selfie after selfie with the galloping horse.

Once we leave the lights of Albuquerque behind, Terrance places his hand in my lap and says, It's such a beautiful night. Look at that moon. Let's stop in Santa Fe on the way.

Absolutely not. I boycott Santa Fe.

You've got to be kidding me. How can you boycott a city?

I don't answer but drive on.

He can tell something is up, so he eyeballs me like *Don't make me ask you.* He possesses the kind of unwavering stare that puts even Metal Matt to shame.

I say, It's like a joke. My dad said he only went there to pick up work or white women.

Um, that's gross.

But, sadly, true. He met my mom there.

Thankfully, he says, and grabbed the hair on the back of my head, lovingly and hard. The moon is almost full, and blue light fills the car. Beautiful, but eerie in a way.

I say, I was born there too. My mom lived with a bunch of other women in some Santa Fe collective house. She gave birth to me in the middle of the living room, surrounded by her friends, while my dad was outside drinking Tecates and grilling carne asada.

That's sweet.

Not really. She told him to leave. But he refused, and he set up outside with a couple of his homies, yelling every now and then to find out if I was a boy or girl.

Terrance says, Why is that, in some fucked-up way, kind of adorable?

He tries to kiss my neck but fails because the seat belt chokes him.

I snicker and say, It was adorable until the point my mom had to call the cops on him. When he found out I was a boy, the party got outta hand.

I barely remember my parents' relationship, but I always

knew it was manic. Every story either one of them told always included screaming and drinking or laughing and loud music. Just thinking about it, my body tensed, like preparing for a fight, like sensing a threat. I'm thankful my mother left my father behind for good when I was little.

Terrance says, Tell me something beautiful about your father.

I stare out at the darkness and the illuminated desert.

I say, He loved New Mexico. The land. The geology of it. The flat-lying rock layers, all red and white and tan sandstone or shale or limestone. The way they eroded and became mesas and buttes. The flora of the desert too, the blooming autumn sage and the Apache plume.

Terrance says, Chino, that is simply a wonderful story. And I bet he loved you too.

I say, You never quite know with fathers, am I right?

Terrance shakes his head. He says, So what are you trying to do with this trip, Chino? Why'd you want to come? Is it the service? Your relatives?

I say, I don't really know. I've lost so much these last few years: my child, my marriage, now my father. I lost my mother so long ago. I'm all alone. I know I'm not, but I kind of am now.

He asks, Were your mom and dad good after things ended?

I say, Like were they friends? Not really. But they didn't hate each other. They just had different plans. The only thing I think they agreed on was my nickname: Chino.

We drive on for about thirty miles until we come to the Black Mesa Travel Center, a fancy name for a gas station with a casino and a diner. I always get the pork taco there, with green chile, topped with shredded iceberg lettuce and pale diced tomatoes.

But more importantly, the place serves the best damn sopapillas anywhere, accompanied by that sticky plastic bear full of honey.

We order four sopapillas and two tacos. The diner serves Pepsi in thirty-two-ounce cups, the red plastic kind, with free refills. When the food arrives, we watch each other while we eat the tacos first: the green chile is superhot. Terrance's eyes water. He keeps wiping them with a napkin from the dispenser. Me, I let myself go, let the heat and the burn cause tear after tear to run down my face. I don't wipe one away. After, we slather the sopapillas in golden honey and lick our fingers clean like kids.

Terrance goes to the bathroom, and when he returns, he shows me a picture of the wall with all this dirty graffiti etched into it.

He says, Why is this so hot and dirty and gross at the same time?

Because you're a perv, I say.

Stop flirting, he says.

We drive for a while without talking. The moon hangs high over the desert. Somber. Slightly spooky. Like something might jump out and scare you.

As we get close to the outskirts of Santa Fe, I say, You wanna hear something hella creepy?

Tell me, he says.

My placenta is buried in this area. We can even cruise by the house that's been built on top of it. My mom cut it in half to make placenta pills. But then she gave the rest to my father, who drove out here and buried it. It was just open desert then—none of these developments had been built.

Terrance says, Wait, she cut it up where? In the kitchen? I'm trying to imagine whipping out the cutting board to carve up your placenta.

I make vomiting sounds, like *Please, say no more.*

He continues, And your dad was like: Hey, cool, let me just bury this somewhere in the desert. Your parents were freaky.

I look at him.

He looks at me and says, And I like.

I shrug and exit the highway.

I turn left onto Dinosaur Trail Road and drive past a smattering of housing subdivisions and soft, undulating mounds covered in shimmering silvery foliage, maybe big sage or saltbush.

The last time I was on this road, I was visiting my father. I was maybe ten. He wanted to reveal to me the exact place he buried it. His crazy plan was to knock on the door and ask the residents if they felt their house was haunted, if they knew they'd bought a house that was built on a buried placenta. I was horrified that he might actually go through with it, and I pleaded for him not to. My father looked at me and shook his head and didn't say a word as he wheeled the car back to the highway and drove all the way to his place in Vegas.

I park across the street from the house.

Terrance turns to me and says, What do you want to do?

He tries to pull me to him, but the Mustang's bucket seats prevent any kind of physical intimacy. Plus, I'm not sure I want to let him hold me. I'm not sure I need anything. I want to do something, but I don't know what it is.

I step out of the car and walk around to the passenger side. I imagine pulling Terrance to me, I imagine squeezing him, but when I open the door, the illuminated horse appears racing across the desert sand.

Holy shit. That's got to be a sign, Terrance says as he bolts from the car and sprints away into the wide-open space across from the cul-de-sac. I watch his body jump this way and that. I hear him calling: *Baby Chino. Come here, baby Chino. Where are you?*

I run after him, loving the way the earth holds on to our every footstep. When I catch up, we're both huffing. He looks at me in the blue moonlight, breathing heavy and hard. He puts his finger to his lips: *Shush.* I hold my breath and close my eyes and feel the pounding of my heart. He places his hands on my face. Delicate. Tender.

Something makes a noise, and we both quickly look. Then we exhale, laugh. We howl. We hold hands and jump up and down. The sand emanates the daytime warmth. I drop, pushing my fingers into it. I look out at the world spreading away from us, smell the earthiness, hear the hum of passing cars on the freeway.

I remember the last time I saw my father. I stayed with him for a week over Christmas the year before Luna got pregnant. Luna had remained in Seattle because I thought it would be just me and my father. But, of course, he had a new girlfriend living with him, so we had almost no time alone together. The last morning, I woke early to catch my flight. I entered his room while they slept. I didn't kiss him goodbye. But I placed my hand on his chest: The rattling breath. The slow beating heart. Proof of being alive, of a living body.

I yank Terrance down to me. He looks at me like *Relax*, but

I shush him and rub my lips gently across his. I stick the tip of my tongue out to lick them. I taste honey and something salty. I laugh, because that's like almost the biggest cliché possible: honey lips. Or sugar lips. Or lips like sugar. I know that's the line to some '80s new wave song. Metal Matt would know. Then I remember Terrance is an '80s music lover, I remember him dancing to the Go-Go's on our first date.

I sing, *Lips like sugar.*

He immediately responds, *Sugar kisses.*

The whole moment feels magical and childlike, exactly what I need. Like maybe next, I might come across a wild desert horse or discover the very spot my father buried the placenta.

I relinquish Terrance and start digging. I flick sand and earth up into the air. Terrance starts to help. We dig little holes here and there, not really trying to find anything, but digging nonetheless.

After a few minutes, we both stop.

Terrance says, Do you believe in ghosts?

No, I say, I don't believe in ghosts. But I guess I believe things can haunt you.

Terrance says, If you let them. If you hold on to them.

Terrance stands and pats off the sand caking his sweatsuit. He then announces: We tried to find him, but it looks like little baby Chino is gone.

I say, He is gone. Chino is gone . . .

The words repeat in my head over and over. I study the desert floor, my half-hearted attempt to look for something, to unearth, to rediscover.

I stand and say, You know. I don't think I want to be called Chino anymore. I want to be called Efren.

Terrance puts his hand on my shoulder, spins me, and dusts off the sand from my ass.

He spins me back to face him and says, Goodbye, Chino. Welcome home, Efren.

He says it with flair and some formality.

I say, Thank you. It's good to be here.

I lean against him, wrap my arms around him. I let myself drop to my knees, wanting to be filled, wanting power and control, desperate to be appreciated, to be loved. Without rushing, I slowly slip down his elastic waistband. He's not wearing underwear. I look up to him, and he smirks in this adorable way. I take him in my mouth, so warm and soft and squishy. I crave that ability to make something so defenseless into something rigid and ungiving, to feel a person become desperately alive. He makes soft sounds, guttural and full of surprise and pleasure. I stare into his face, and to witness such desire, let me tell you, it's like leaving everything that I don't need behind and discovering everything that I do.

I stop and stand. His eyes look into mine. He kisses me.

I say, Call me Efren.

Terrance whispers, Efren, and the way he says it, like he's desperate for more, thrills me.

Say it again louder.

Efren.

Louder.

Efrennnnnnnn! Terrance belts out into the silence, into the wild, wild world.

I walk away from him and stroll to the car, my urgency gone. I take my time getting settled behind the wheel. As I drive up to the freeway, I head south, back to Albuquerque, instead of north, toward the high desert, to Las Vegas, where my father's body is about to be laid to rest.

So, Efren. Change of plans?

I say, I found what I was looking for.

From *Ferns of Northern California*

Live oaks thrive along the Northern California coastline—from Oakland to Eureka—and so, too, does the resurrection fern, which grows on their trunks and branches. For most of the late spring through summer and into fall, resurrection ferns appear dead and brown, with a crispy texture. Yet come the first few days of rain, at the outset of winter, they burst into life, lush and green, enveloping each of the tree's branches in fuzzy, verdant life—a cycle that repeats itself, over and over again.

A FEW WEEKS have passed since I returned from New Mexico. I started seeing a therapist named River, which makes me smirk, like *Really?* His office in Forestville sits across the street from the Forestville Club, where Genevieve and I had our first date. I talk about feeling uncomfortable when I have a good time. He calls it survivor's guilt. I call it shame. He asks: What are you ashamed of? I haven't quite answered that yet, but I think it's about my desire to forget.

He's this strangely fit—like he must play some kind of sport—fiftyish white dude, but something about his jockyness makes palatable his new-agey vibe. I like the contradiction.

I've given notice to my after-school job and my rental, both of which now end on January 1. I found a small basement in-law unit in Metal Matt's neighborhood, with a two-bedroom house above me, but the best thing is the backyard: ignored and a bit feral, with rogue lemon and plum trees and several failed attempts at garden boxes scattered through, a little oasis.

My grand plan: Come summer, open enrollment for Oakland Wilds Science Classes for Kids. My own business, my way.

Genevieve invites me to her cabin on my last Sunday in Guerneville for a late lunch: her legendary spaghetti. It's a cold December afternoon, so I'm bundled up when I enter, and I immediately can tell Genevieve feels frisky, because she's wearing a floral linen dress, despite the chill in the cabin. She tells me to stand behind her as she chops onions. To breathe on her neck. To gently and slowly lift up the hem of her dress.

Stop, she says then, and makes me sit in a chair. She hands me a mason jar of red wine and starts telling me random stories about dropping out of high school, helping to organize antiglobalization actions in the '90s, and starting the local chapter of Copwatch.

I chuckle and say, You like to watch cops too.

She looks at me, her eyes unblinking, focused, calculating. I feel small and delicious.

When the meal is ready, she asks, Are you hungry? The tenor of her words is somewhere close to a demand.

I say, Starving.

She hitches up the dress and pulls down her underwear—purple cotton, nothing fancy—stepping out of them, leaving them on the floor. I catch a glimpse of her pubic hair.

She tells me to follow her. She places two chairs facing each other and motions me to sit. She hands me a plate piled with spaghetti and covered in thick marinara sauce. Since there's no table, I hold the plate with one hand and the fork with the other. She sits across from me and spreads her legs.

Feed yourself, she says.

At first, I try to eat with delicate bites, worrying about how I might look, wondering if the sauce gathers in the crevices of my mouth.

It's wonderful, so rich and tangy. I give in. I slurp up noodles. I notice the sauce fling this way and that. Genevieve's hand strokes her pussy, matching the rhythm of my chewing. Her eyes are round and wide.

Lying in bed after, I feel completely satiated and safe. She vapes her postdate THC, her exhalations smelling of citrus candy.

So, you want to be called Efren, not Chino? Genevieve asks, like she's confused and wants to understand. She has a very particular routine at the end of our dates: Brief pillow talk, while getting high, then she dresses in a terry-cloth robe and watches me put on my clothes and shoes. When I'm dressed, she escorts me to the door by the hand. But tonight, I can tell she's feeling generous, probably because this will be the last time we hang out for the foreseeable future.

I say, Yes, like cleansing the body. A new me. Leave all the old shit behind.

You think changing your name will do that?

I say, It's not just changing my name. It's taking charge.

She giggles, and her laughter begins to pick up speed. Her body shakes, and I grin, watching her breasts move. She notices and grabs them.

She says, See these stretch marks? That's from raising babies. I love these reminders, sweetie.

She sits up on her elbows and says, I don't know why everybody wants to leave their baggage behind. I don't want to leave anything behind. I want to take everything with me.

She lies back down and touches her stomach, lined with jagged, faded stretch marks running from her belly button to her pubic hair. I love it when she calls me *sweetie*. I raise my hand and stick out my finger and lick the tip of it and then trace one of the lines, slowly, down her body. I lick my finger again and trace another one. And another. She watches me the whole time, with

an eagerness. She then pulls my head to her chest, and I take one
nipple in my mouth.

Good for you, she says. Seems like 2020 is going to be your
year.

She sits and picks up her robe, which I know means the date
is over.

I walk the darkening roads back to my cabin: A quarter mile,
a cold night coming, but right now it's clear and calm, sunset
peeking through overhead branches, everything smelling of
recent rain and damp earth. I hear my footsteps squish on the
wet redwood needles that drop every fall.

As I approach my cabin, Mr. Garofalo sits on his stoop, just
up the hill from me, watching the day come to an end. I wave.

I say, Hey, I got a few extra beers you can have.

I bring him a box of Modelos, and he asks if I want one.

I sit and say, You've been a great neighbor. Thanks for the
help when I first moved in.

What else is a neighbor supposed to do? he says, and sips his
beer.

He asks, You know who's moving in?

He says it like I better make sure it's not an asshole.

We sit together and drink our beer, and I think of moving.
When I was a child, my mother moved me constantly—from
Albuquerque to Las Cruces to El Paso to Sedona to Flagstaff and
about six other cities—until death caught up with her at Goleta,
on the coast of California. Every time we'd pack for a new place,
she'd sing: *A new chance, a new chap.* Which I assumed were
lyrics from some pop song she loved.

But I never confirmed that.

I spent my eighteenth birthday in a hospice home, watching *Home Improvement* and *3rd Rock from the Sun* episodes on VHS, missing most of my final semester of high school.

Perhaps Genevieve is right. All your pain and all your joy. All the ridiculous memories and regrets and mistakes: Why would you want to leave all those memories of family and friends and broken hearts and birth and death behind?

PART THREE

Spring 2020–Fall 2022

2020 Is Going to Be My Year

AS YOU KNOW, the world changed. 2020 was absolutely no one's year.

Nothing worked out as planned.

And yet. Here I am: Efren Chino Flores.

Still.

I can't hide under the arrogance of present tense, that assurance of possibility. Life doesn't work like that.

Here's what happened. I'm holding on to all of it. Every single thing.

I saw the dog first. It looked friendly: about forty pounds, brindled and thin. Then the homemade leash, made of what looked like yellow nylon rope, knotted to the security gate outside China Gourmet on Foothill Boulevard.

The dog didn't bark, but it didn't look happy either. As usual, Fruitvale was a mess with commuter traffic, engines blaring, all the headlights and blinking brake lights, the noise of angry drivers trying to get someplace right at six o'clock. Plus that night, the world felt strange. The shelter-in-place order would go into effect the next day.

Each sound provoked this cringe and whine in the poor animal. I empathized with the dog, because those were the times that I missed my cabin in the redwoods, my quiet river walks, my solitude. I had moved back to the Bay, to Oakland to be closer to Metal Matt, and now: lockdown.

It would just be me in my apartment, alone.

I knew I should have gone to get groceries, but I couldn't face the rush of shoppers and that wild, nervous energy. Instead, self-care: an order of Chinese food and a few beers at my new studio. As I entered China Gourmet, I cooed at the dog: Good dog.

Its face looked at me like *What's good about me?*

The gruff older lady called Auntie worked the counter. I had hoped for the younger, nicer one. I'm sure she treated everyone like this, but every time I ordered, regardless of what it was, she made a big deal to give me an extra couple pieces of orange chicken or beef and broccoli. She'd say, Here you go, love.

Being called *love* and getting a few extra pieces: What more could a person want?

The gruff Auntie, busy counting change and stacking it into little towers, didn't look up when I stepped to the counter, so I acted like I was trying to decide, when I knew exactly what I wanted.

I stood there waiting, and I felt the dog staring at me.

The restaurant was stark white with red booths and tables, like a fast-food restaurant might have been there originally. But the owners had added an inch-thick glass security barrier between us and all the food. There were only two booths: the one close to the door held a couple of teen boys dressed in beige pants and white polo shirts, the uniform of the charter school up the street. They talked excitedly about the fact that school was canceled indefinitely.

The man at the second booth, with a half-eaten egg roll in front of him next to a little plastic cup of fluorescent-red dipping sauce, drank a tall boy Tecate. He wore a neon-blue backpack, half unzipped, stuffed with one of those Oakland A's plush blankets.

The lady looked up, and I ordered. She wanted me to pay the $5.75 before she made my plate. I gave her $6 and waited for her to give me back the quarter. I made a big deal of dropping it into the tip jar as she slowly plated my food.

There were only four pieces of chicken on it, so I asked for more.

She said: What? Like she didn't understand why.

I explained: There's just four pieces. There should be at least six.

She shrugged and—holding eye contact with me—proceeded to place two more pieces on my plate.

When I turned around, the guy with the egg roll had abandoned his booth, so I slid in to quickly eat my food.

I watched him standing at the door, holding his beer with one hand and trying to untie the dog with the other. The dog backed into the restaurant, away from the man, pulling at the leash. He slapped the cowering animal and yelled: Brucebruce.

I'm not sure if he spoke English or Spanish, but either way, Brucebruce had to be the worst dog name ever. Brucebruce did this weird jump and yelp and knocked into the man's beer, which thudded to the ground and rolled to the gutter leaving a foamy white trail.

I shook my head and focused on my plate, forking up the perfect balance of salty noodles and sweet lemon chicken. But before I could get my next bite ready, chaos erupted. The man must have tripped retrieving his beer, because people started gathering around a figure lying on the sidewalk. The teens raced to the door, filming with their phones. The dog jumped around, agitated, as a bystander stepped into the restaurant and demanded hielo. Auntie handed her a bag so quickly I was impressed, like they were a team. A voice shouted something in Spanish I couldn't quite understand, so I stood, instinctually, to look, but I sat back down because the last thing I wanted to see was someone hurt or in pain.

This was not how I wanted to eat my last meal before lockdown. I picked up my plate and walked to the counter and asked for a to-go box. The Auntie said: It's a quarter.

I said: Really?

She nodded her head like *Obviously, yes.*

I wanted to reach into the tip jar and grab my quarter back, but I knew better. I gave her a dollar, and she reached into the tip jar, handed me three quarters, and dropped the bill inside.

I placed the food in the box and walked out of the restaurant, stepping around the people milling near the entrance. I saw Brucebruce, still tied up and huddled outside, trembling—trying to get away from it all. I opened the box and gave him one of my five remaining pieces of chicken. I said: Good dog.

He looked at me like *Yes, you should.*

So I did. I reached down and yanked on the nylon knot till it loosened just enough. Brucebruce backed out of the noose.

The dog ran. No hesitation. No fear. He barreled away through the stopped traffic with impressive agility, and a prance that made me feel like a winner. Like soon the cars will clear and everything will move smoothly again. Like the man on the sidewalk will be fine. Like this pandemic will end. Like the next time I enter China Gourmet, I'll get six pieces of chicken without even having to ask.

To Sing Perverted Songs Out Loud Together

AFTER THE FIRST three months of the shelter-in-place order, the only people in my life were:

Terrance, who lived in a cute bungalow in Glendale with his new partner, Marco. We set up a weekly Zoom Boom Night (his name for it), during which we played a couple rounds of blackjack or poker while we gossiped, and then sometimes we engaged in a dirty-talking masturbatory session. I suspected sometimes Marco watched off to the side. Maybe it was their thing. Terrance definitely had a thing for setting. He'd don his velour robe, and we'd set up the laptop camera in the corner of different rooms: the kitchen, the backyard, or the bathroom. He definitely loved bathroom hookups. I missed his energy, his round face and body and belly.

Kay and Mike, who had just left the city for the other side of Lake Merritt. They'd moved into a two-sided duplex with a yard, because they didn't want to be trapped in their one-room apartment in Richmond, with its ever-present cold and gray skies. They'd canceled their wedding plans, both agreeing that money might be an issue for a while. I remember chiding them, sure that they were wrong. We'd meet up to walk the lake, struggling to remain the mandated six feet apart.

And, of course, Metal Matt, often accompanied by Suzi. In a Covid-induced romantic gesture, Metal Matt had invited Suzi to hunker down with him and Sabbath at his apartment in Oakland.

Metal Matt and I had a standing biweekly Covid meet-up at Peralta Park on Coolidge Avenue, our coolers containing, depending on the time of day or night, either LaCroix or a selection of kombucha beverages. We'd worry about infection data and spikes. We'd reminisce about indoor dining and going to shows. Often, we'd discuss money issues and jobs: Metal Matt's sound-engineering gigs for events ended overnight. My science classes, initially on hold, were set to start in a few months, outdoors only.

Suzi's work was already online pre-pandemic, but members of her collective workspace canceled when the lockdown stretched into its second month. She broached the subject with Metal Matt about inviting me, Kay, and Mike to join, offering a discounted rate, just enough to afford the space through the lockdown. In the meantime, she organized a weekly Zoom happy hour hangout each Thursday in order to get to know everyone. After the first meeting, Suzi announced that the chat records would be saved for corroboration about attendance and any other agreements, as if that were an added incentive to become a member.

The Zoom dates and shared worry helped me feel needed and a part of something larger. But at the end of each day, I was always alone in my apartment.

The one other person I was in contact with: River, my therapist. During our weekly Zoom sessions, he always wore some colorful, comfy-looking sweater, and he had always had large houseplants in his background and a huge window through which I could see redwood trunks. He supported the choices I'd been making in the moments when things got stressful (mostly drinking), but he also steered me back to what we had earlier in our sessions decided was important to me: health, community, joy, forgiveness.

I loved this: having someone remind me over and over what mattered to me.

For our meetings, he required me to not only put on pants and a belt, but shoes and socks. And he required proof. I also loved being held accountable.

One day, after our check-ins about coping choices to the unprecedented communal stress we are all under (his description), he asked: So what's something unexpected that's brought you some joy, some light, this week?

I said, Okay, so during my nightly postdrinking hours before sleep—usually premasturbation—I recently discovered these strange videos on YouTube.

He said, I love to hear about masturbation. He snorted and laughed, and—I couldn't help it—I laughed right along with him.

He said, You know what I mean. Masturbation is healthy and should be talked about more freely. And not to dismiss your comment about alcohol, but everyone's drinking a little bit too much, so be easy on yourself.

I said, I know, but my father gave me one good piece of advice: Don't become an addict. So I'm perhaps a bit too anxious about my drinking.

I hear you. Sounds like good advice. Do you want to talk about addiction or your father?

Not really.

Then tell me about those videos.

I said, There are these videos of professional voice coaches listening to metal bands and commenting on how amazing the singers are to hit those notes while contorting their bodies.

I sat upright on my couch, remembering the videos of the coaches leaning forward, stunned and perplexed and astounded by the singers, who are writhing or bouncing or hunched over in something like ecstasy.

I heard my therapist ask, And this brings you joy?

I said, Yes. But it gets better.

I leaned in to my Zoom camera and lowered my voice like I was one of those voice coaches. River smiled when he saw me.

I said, I discovered this whole subgenre of Christian couples or Christian fathers and sons listening to Nine Inch Nails or Tool for the first time. All this revulsion and camaraderie they shared, the look on their faces: pure arrogant self-righteousness.

River asked, So seeing their shared experience pleases you?

I closed my eyes and imagined their faces: It was so voyeuristic, even erotic, like you were witnessing intimacy right as it was created between two people. It was so hot—their bond and excitement over hating something I loved. I watched video after video, drank glass after glass, until I ended up making myself cum sitting on the living room couch. With all the lights on, right hand holding my wine, mouth open, lips stained red, I'd sing along to "Closer" or "Stinkfist," playing with myself with my left hand as the YouTubers repeatedly stopped and shared their analysis of the offensive lyrics, their voices all appalled and indignant.

Right then, I realized how much I missed the way I felt with Luna or Terrance or Leila or Genevieve in the afterglow of a sexual act. It wasn't the sex I missed.

It was the tenderness, the silence, the hushed breathing, when all pretensions disappeared, the roles, the toys, and we just were there together—sometimes touching, sometimes talking, sometimes silent, but together.

I opened my eyes and looked at the screen. My image startled me: my skin flushed and beautiful.

I looked alive.

I TRIED TO relay my epiphany to Metal Matt. We sat in the glow of a warm summer afternoon: Peralta Park empty, the kids' playground closed off by yellow caution tape, the threat of infection everywhere.

I said, I figured it out. What I want in a partner.

Share with me please, he said, and scratched Sabbath's head preemptively, noticing that the dog was about to growl at some arrogant crow daring to land in the field.

I said, I want someone to get naked and join me on the couch with my laptop and a bottle of wine. I want to YouTube with them. I want to pause videos and banter judgmental commentary. To sing perverted songs out loud together—I want all of that.

He said, Um, disturbingly specific, but I get it.

So why's it so damn hard to find?

I have no idea, but have you told actually anyone that's what you want? Besides me.

I can only imagine writing that on my Tinder profile: looking for someone to get naked and watch YouTube videos with.

Bet you'd be inundated by a bunch of metal freaks.

Two people in masks approached our beach chairs. Yet once they saw us, they made such a wide berth that Sabbath didn't even bother to bark.

How's living with Suzi?

I love it. But check this out.

Metal Matt turned in his chair like he was about to reveal something juicy.

She can't sleep in the same bed as me. She waits for me to fall asleep and then moves to the couch. Like what the hell. Should I be offended?

You know you do snore, right?

He didn't even bother to respond.

I asked, Does it bother you?

It does. Just a little bit—it does.

Tell her, I said.

Tell her she can't leave the bed because it bothers me? Nah, it doesn't matter. I'm superthankful for our connection, but long-term, who knows what will happen once all this ends in a few months. It can't go on much longer.

Masks Up, Pants Down

FIVE MONTHS INTO the pandemic, we were all coming to terms with the fact that things weren't going to magically return to normal anytime soon. So we—Kay, Mike, Metal Matt, Suzi and I—agreed to be a pod. To be maskless around each other and masked around everyone else. If one of us was compromised or came into close contact with someone outside of the pod, we agreed to wait the CDC-mandated ten days before returning to the fold. It was a bit creepy and exclusive, but it felt safe, just the five of us.

We created a group text dubbed The Five Podsketeers. Of course, I was the proverbial fifth podsketeer, because Kay and Mike and Suzi and Metal Matt all shared more than just aerosol particulates with each other. We all met up to tour Suzi's collective workspace in person on East Twenty-Third and Fruitvale, and we each agreed to pay $200 a month for rent and upkeep once things returned to a semblance of normal. We were all there: one big happy Covid pod.

The space was on the second floor, above a laundromat converted into a makeshift Pentecostal church space. It served mostly Central Americans, and no one from the collective ever worked there on Sundays, because the service was riotous.

The floor plan was relatively simple: a kitchenette with white linoleum flooring and a laminate countertop, a dark single-user bathroom, and enough space for us each to have our own desk separated by cheap OfficeMax portable wall dividers. The configuration allowed everyone to enjoy the light shining through the long windows along the Fruitvale side.

Unmasked but still trying to remain six feet apart, we bantered over who got what: Kay needed space to spread out her fiction thesis, as an MFA professor had recommended. Mike wanted a corner office, so he could edit his printed-out tech documents in natural light, rather than the blue light of the computer screen—demand for his editorial services had exploded, thanks to Covid. Metal Matt and Suzi already had claimed their sections pre-pandemic. So my spot was the back corner—with no windows, but closest to the bathroom, the kitchenette, and the communal area.

I said, So I'm assuming the communal area will have some pinball and a selection of kombucha on draft. Like Google or Salesforce?

Suzi said, It will have a working fridge in which you can refrigerate your own beverages of choice.

I said, I'll take it.

❧

LIFE HAD A lonely, comfortable rhythm to it, until Genevieve texted for the first time since I left Guerneville. She said: Listen, I'm staying in Berkeley to help with my grandchild. Want to social-distance hook up?

I was a bit apprehensive, but of course I agreed.

The night before our date, I dreamed of bodies and scents. I dreamed of leaning into her neck and sniffing. I imagined raising her arms and breathing in her natural smell. I imagined unzipping her pants and inhaling her into me. I also dreamed of blackjack and Terrance, of cards sliding across a verdant green felt table and me knocking the table twice, demanding *Hit me,* with a smile.

We got two Manhattans in mason jars from the window of a bar called Revival and walked around the empty streets of downtown Berkeley bundled to fight the unseasonably chilly summer afternoon. But Genevieve wasted little time, which I appreciated. She explained the rules: I don't want to get Covid, she said. So no touching, just watching.

I stared at her: black mask bedazzled with plastic jewels, a red-and-white blouse, and a denim skirt with black yoga pants.

I stepped to her, pulling my mask down below my nose, ready to breathe her in.

She stepped back: Did you hear? No touching. Let's drive into the Kittredge parking garage.

As I pulled up to her white Camry, I revved my Ford Ranger: *rrrrrr rrrrrr,* a satisfying purr. Through her rear window, I could see she had a child's car seat in the back.

Grandchild? I asked.

Shh, she said, and drove away toward the entrance.

The fully automated garage had a good number of cars on level one and two, but level three had only a smattering, just enough for us not to look too suspicious. She raced ahead to a corner parking spot and backed into it, waving for me to do the same, shouting out the window to leave six feet distance between. We killed our engines, got out, and stood apart. I waited: she pressed her legs together and slid down the yoga pants.

The first and only time she touched me: when she reached out to find balance as each foot pulled free.

She said: Get in your truck and crack the window so you can hear me.

She pulled the skirt up and slipped her underwear down, then balled it up and tossed it into the back of her car. I watched the underwear land perfectly in the car seat.

She growled, Go. And I went.

I got in and turned to face her. I cracked the window, and she slipped the elastic off one ear. It was the sexiest thing I'd ever seen: mask dangling, full lips, and teeth all white and square.

She said: Lean back and spread your legs for me. I want to see everything.

I grinned and shrugged, like *Okay.*

I tried to lean sideways in this slow and sexy way against the dashboard and smiled.

Lie down on the seat, she demanded.

I scooted my butt forward and squeezed in between the gear shift and the seat and discovered that my dome light was on. I worried for a second about my battery but remembered I had my jumper cables with me.

I yanked my pants off. I placed my feet on the top edges of the window. I spread myself open. I felt vulnerable and on display, like I was being inspected for approval.

I loved it.

My body felt new: the soft fur of my ass cheeks, the shameful excitement, knowing my asshole was exposed and visible, my cock starting to thrum and pulse and fill out, the way my balls nestled and fit so perfectly between my raised legs.

I held the position and waited.

I could hear her breathing and murmuring words I couldn't quite understand. She got louder and louder, and I knew she was cumming.

I sat up to watch as she leaned back against her car, the look on her face—such satisfaction, such happiness.

I watched the soft, slow way she stroked herself, her fingernails painted bright blue, her pubic hair untrimmed and full between her fingers.

She finished, then pushed down her skirt and slipped on her mask.

I said: Wait—give me your hand. Please.

She stepped to the window, and three delicate fingers slid into my car. I moved my face right in front of them, feeling a rush of fear, of possible infection. I sniffed like the scent could save my life and closed my eyes in appreciation. I stuck out my tongue and licked the tip of each finger.

She said wait five minutes before you leave. I'll text you later.

Then, I heard her car start and the squeal of rubber on painted cement as she drove off.

No matter, I thought.

I considered my cock and my balls and my thighs. I could see my pants and my underwear, a messy bundle at my feet. I felt satiated, calm, relaxed.

I thought, *How sexy is this.*

How perfect.

I looked divine.

I waited even longer than five minutes before I drove myself home.

Balls and Stars

I STARTED TAKING long strolls around my neighborhood, always aimless, just walking away from my place on Thirty-Fifth and Paxton. Pre-pandemic, I never walked anywhere if I didn't have to. I loved my beat-up truck and would even drive the half mile to the Mexican markets that dotted Fruitvale Ave between MacArthur and International.

The markets usually had everything in stock, while the larger grocery chains were uniformly pillaged by the Oakland Hills residents who were too concerned about their health to come to the crowded and impossible-to-social-distance-in shops throughout East Oakland.

But lately, walking felt glorious, something to dress for, to take a look in the mirror for, to primp and pose. My hair was puffy and as full as it had ever been in my life.

I explored side streets and neighborhood parks. I appreciated the city-sponsored Slow Streets, which were off-limits to cars. Every time I discovered one, I saw kids biking and playing, elders walking leisurely. People even set up chairs to sit outside and safely gather with neighbors.

I'd always stop at Foothill and Fruitvale to buy sliced mango covered in Tajin and lime, from a masked young man with a fruit cart. I'd get street tacos on Twenty-Sixth Avenue, a side street off of Fruitvale, where Oakland PD always hassled the vendors about fire safety. I'd relax in Josie de la Cruz Park, with its miniature soccer field.

One evening, I sat in the grass and listened to this group of kids talking shit in Spanish. They had ripped down the DO NOT ENTER caution tape meant to prevent people from gathering on playgrounds and sports fields. They had reclaimed this public space, unmasked, living out a physical closeness I didn't have but painfully craved.

I eyed this one kid as he picked up a soda can and threw it at a dog, missing him by inches. It was awful. And I stared in disbelief, because I was sure it was the same dog I'd freed the night before the lockdown. His name came right back to me: Brucebruce. The last time we'd encountered each other, he had raced through traffic on Foothill.

The dog very casually sauntered out of range and sat waiting the teenagers out. I left the park thinking, *Good for him.* I was glad the dog had survived—he was making this work, like all of us. I even felt a little responsible for it.

The next time Metal Matt and I hung out, I told him the story of how I had liberated this dog called Brucebruce from its abusive owner right as the pandemic started, thinking he'd be impressed by my act of kindness.

But he was aghast. Like how could I just let some animal run wild on the busy streets of East Oakland and think, in any way, that what I'd done was a good thing?

He shook his head and pulled Sabbath toward himself, cooing: I'll always protect you, Sabbath Bloody Sabbath, especially from Evil Efren.

You know that's a dumb nickname.

It's the title of Black Sabbath's fifth album, arguably their best. How's that dumb?

It was still dumb, but he was right about Brucebruce. How arrogant was I to free an animal and yet to take no responsibility for its safety? Despite my best intentions, I might have put the dog in even more danger out on his own.

I frowned, self-loathing surging through my body, as I thought about how often my actions were selfish.

I wasn't brave enough to call my father back when he asked me to. As I'd witnessed Luna cradling our child's body—the nurses and the doula reverent and ceremonial—I'd refused to hold or even look at the baby.

☙

THAT VERY NIGHT the kittens showed up at my door.

I stepped out into my backyard at 3 a.m. because something kept yowling and whining. I opened the door ready to shoo the thing away, and two baby cats, one orange and one gray, pranced inside like they lived there and were returning home from a joyous night out.

At first, I was aggravated, like *Get out of my space,* but the orange one rolled over, and I could see his cute little balls, soft and furry, in an adorable oval shape. The gray one raced up and swatted the other kitten feebly. I fed them some chicken I had left over from my favorite spot: Lucky Three Seven. They have the best wings, covered in this sauce called G Fire, which I know must have way too much sugar in it. But, anyway, I should've known the kittens would be like: *Hell yeah, we gonna live here.* They snuggled up at the foot of my bed and slept like they were the safest little forest creatures in the world.

After a couple weeks of giving them human food, I broke down and bought canned cat food and kitty litter and made an appointment at the outdoor free vet clinic. But when the vet tech asked their names, I realized I never considered them mine, because who names a cat Ratty and Balls. I'd named them that to make fun of them, not to love them.

Ratty and Balls, the vet tech said. Like he was clarifying the names.

He was dressed head to foot in PPE attire, so I only saw his eyes.

Yes, I enunciated through my mask.

Okay then, but Balls better enjoy his for the next hour—he's about to have them in name only.

His balls were the soft yellow of unripe apricots. I felt a pang of regret. Not that I'd named him Balls, but that I'd brought him here to lose them.

It had been a hard year. I felt the need to hold on to such tiny precious things.

I bragged to Metal Matt at Peralta Park that I was making amends for releasing Brucebruce by fostering these two feral kittens, but I complained how they never really let me pick them up and spent most of their time racing through my apartment chasing crumpled-up Post-it notes.

Metal Matt said, You mean the cats play fetch?

They don't fetch. They're cats, not dogs, I said.

Do you throw these crumpled Post-it notes?

Yes.

And do the cats bring them back to you?

Yes.

You have cats that play fetch. Do you let them outside?

At night, when I go out. They follow me, but then they always come back inside.

When I told Terrance over Zoom about the cats, he said, Ah, you're one of those people who got quarantine pets. I read an article about it. It's apparently a thing that lonely people do.

I'm not lonely.

Do you have a quarantine pet?

No. I have a consensual relationship with two abandoned cats that have adopted me.

They must've known.

Known what?

Known that you're lonely. And that's okay. We all are, really.

ONE NIGHT IN December, I stepped into the backyard to witness the planetary convergence that everyone was posting about. I had a cup of tea. I let Balls and Ratty out, watched them sprint away into the darkness. I heard the side gate bang open and closed, and was about to shout *Get out* when my upstairs neighbors, a young couple—Jas and Jan—walked into the yard and waved at me. I waved back like this was a regular occurrence, but I don't think I'd ever seen them back here. Normally, I saw only one of them or the other when they stepped out their front door to pick up the nonstop deliveries that arrived: takeout, groceries, Amazon boxes.

They searched the sky.

You know the stars are lining up tonight, Jas said, as if I'd asked him to explain his presence. He sounded strangely excited, like this was something he'd been waiting for.

Not stars, babe. Planets, Jan said.

Yes, that's right—planets. Saturn and Mars.

Jupiter, not Mars. Babe, come on, are you just teasing me? she said, and she reached out to push him.

I realized he might have been teasing her. They were cute together.

My cats sauntered up to me and sat at my feet like I'd trained them.

Oh my god. Look, Jas. It's our cats. It's Kurt and Cobain. Where have you two been? We looked all over for you.

She hustled over and picked up Ratty, who meowed like she was so sad and scared.

Balls meowed like he wanted to be picked up. Like I hadn't tried to pick him up every day for weeks.

Jas picked up Balls and cradled him like a little newborn baby, his four little paws reaching skyward.

Jan, all tears and excitement, asked, Have they been with you the whole time?

I said, I thought they were feral.

Jan looked at Jas and said, I told you we should have put up flyers. I knew they were around here.

They raced toward their apartment, forgetting all about the planets and stars.

The cats looked back at me, and just like that, they were gone.

I thought about saying something about their medical records, but, really, what could I say?

I figured Jas would soon find the balls gone and figure it out.

I remained outside and threw the rest of my Post-it notes into the darkness. Every time I threw one, the floodlights went on.

When I was finally out of Post-its, I just sat there listening to the sounds of East Oakland: the tire squeals, BART screeching, a car alarm, the ever-present and year-round pop of fireworks.

I looked up into the sky, and, sure enough, I saw the planets converge. It was a beautiful sight, that bright, steady light that for centuries had guided people home.

Every Homie Needs a Nickname

AFTER RATTY AND Balls abandoned me to live with Jas and Jan, I felt disappointed, but I told myself that they'd left in better shape than they'd arrived (sans Balls's testicles, of course). I even left my extra cans of cat food on Jas and Jan's stoop, though I kept a couple, just in case.

Then, I focused all my attention on the things I had going for me, rather than the things I had lost.

I updated my website for the upcoming expansion of Oakland Wilds. I was going to offer two-hour afternoon classes Monday through Thursday, with up to ten students each. Although federal law allowed up to twelve, I knew my limitations and felt better providing more hands-on instruction. This would double my income. I felt flush. More importantly, I felt like I was doing the right thing.

But I could still feel something missing. Maybe Terrance was right: I needed the cats more than they needed me. Then it dawned on me: *Find Brucebruce. Make it right.* A chance for redemption.

And one day later, like it was kismet, I encountered Brucebruce again at Josie de la Cruz Park. He sat about twenty feet from the soccer team benches, waiting for the inevitable trail of edible rubbish: discarded chicken bones, paper plates with beans and rice. He had this candy wrapper hanging from his muzzle, but he looked good: clean, the whites in his fur still stark, ears up and eager. I had assumed the worst: that he'd be mangy and matted, especially after watching that teenager throw a soda can at him.

Brucebruce, I called, and the dog strolled up to me like we were old friends.

I took off my belt to use as a temporary leash, but Brucebruce bounded backward, ears immediately retracted in distrust. I apologized and put my belt back on. He stepped to me again, ears up, the candy wrapper now gone from his fur.

I wanted to say something important, something that explained everything between us.

I said, Here's the deal. I promise never to tie you up, and you can leave anytime you want to, but if you stay with me, you have to . . .

I didn't know how to finish. I cringed at the word *obey*. I balked at saying *listen to me*. Nothing felt right. The dog cocked his head.

I said, I need you to work with me. How's that?

He said nothing, but he moved closer to me and sat. I reached out cautiously and touched his head. I could feel the soft, slightly grimy hair, the subtle shift in weight as the dog leaned into my hand.

We walked side by side to my backyard. I opened a can of cat food and grabbed a bowl for water. I sat in my backyard chair while Brucebruce ate and then curled up at my feet.

I called Metal Matt.

Be careful. Don't get too attached, like you did with those cats.

Fuck Ratty and Balls, I said.

Of course, Metal Matt said. Fuck 'em.

I said, I want to find him a home. Will you help me?

We made flyers at the workspace. We took a picture of Brucebruce against a white backdrop, his red tongue hanging out of his mouth like he was dying of thirst, text reading: DO YOU KNOW MY PERSON? (*Nothing should be owned,* I thought, after first writing the word *owner.*) We printed them up at the workspace, Suzi and Kay offering their input on how many copies I'd need and where to put them up. Suzi suggested we use painter's tape to be courteous to the walls to which we attached the flyers, while Kay rummaged up a box of tacks to use where appropriate. Team Brucebruce to the rescue, I said as we were about to leave.

Brucebruce sat and watched every time I put up a flyer over the next few days.

If you want to go, I said, you can go.

He said nothing.

I posted flyers around China Gourmet and at all the liquor stores. I taped them to telephone poles, community boards, and bus stops. I emailed a file to all my students' parents. I even knocked on Jas and Jan's door to ask if they recognized him. I pointed to Brucebruce sitting on the sidewalk below, ears up like he was hopeful they would.

Brucebruce always stayed with me. He'd sometimes run

ahead, but he kept to the sidewalks and never ran in the street. That's how I discovered Donut Savant on Thirty-Eighth. I saw a line of people six feet apart stretching an entire block. I started to move along, to cross the street, but Brucebruce stayed put in front of the store. He sniffed the air, and so—what else could I do?—I sniffed: *Ah, the sweet odor of baking dough.*

I wanted to hate the place, but its specialty, cronuts—a cross between a donut and a croissant, drizzled in this perfect vanilla glaze—were divine.

And so, yes, Brucebruce and I began stopping by on our morning walks.

And, yes, we generally were first in line when it opened at eight.

☀

A FEW WEEKS after posting flyers, Brucebruce and I stood in line outside Donut Savant on the stenciled dancing donuts that marked six feet between customers. We were running late this morning. Brucebruce kept walking to the front door and then back to me, like *What are you waiting for?* I shook my head and slapped my thigh, but he walked back to the front door. He repeated this a few times before we finally got to the serving counter.

Hey, boss, all the vanillas are gone, Javier said to me.

He was young and thin and had a smile full of gold teeth, with wild, bushy hair that he kept tied in a loose ponytail.

He knew I always ordered a vanilla cronut, a black coffee, and a dog biscuit. He also knew I had a degree in botany, because I'd started bringing in my after-school class each Thursday to get cronuts as a reward for their hard work identifying ten different kinds of plants in Dimond Park. Javier liked to tease the kids, asking if they could identify which plant the elusive cronut grew on. The kids loved it.

Javier made me slightly giddy. He had this genuine, optimistic energy, like everything was cool, everything would be fine. Sometimes you just want to bask in the possibility of hope and faith of some young person, like nothing could go wrong or get lost or not come to fruition.

He slid me a coffee and walked around the counter and said, Bruceyboy, this one's on me.

You know his name is Brucebruce, I said.

Every little homie needs a nickname, he said, rubbing Brucebruce's head. The dog lifted his head further into the young man's hand.

Javier said, Try something new. The maple one is fire.

I nodded yes, because the warm coffee made me want something sweet.

Boss, let me show you something from my friend's grow?

Sure, I said.

Check this out. He presented me with a marijuana leaf, curled at the edges, with brown circular spots.

Look like mites, I said. You can spray it with a vinegar solution.

We did, he said.

He wanted to know if it's possible to still save them. To get a good harvest. Or is it best to just throw out the whole crop?

I hate to throw anything away, I said. But if your goal is to get the best harvest, I think it's best to start again.

He said, Sometimes you gotta start fresh.

He crumpled the leaf and shot it toward the wastebasket. It floated in.

I smiled at Javier, at his optimism. I held my hot cup of coffee and my maple cronut while Brucebruce crunched his flour bone.

Javier raised his fist, but, seeing my hands full, reached out to pat me on the shoulder.

He walked back behind the counter. Why do you never have Bruceyboy on a leash? he said.

He doesn't like it.

You must be superkind.

Why?

Animals only respect people they know won't hurt them.

I breathed in sharply. It's the nicest thing someone had said to me since before lockdown.

But, Javier added, you need to give him a bath.

❧

THE NEXT MORNING, I stepped into the shower and thought, *Why not?*

I called the dog, who came to the tub.

Join me?

I made room for him, and he put his paws on the rim and jumped into the hot shower. I used my Head & Shoulders combo shampoo and conditioner and lathered him up until he looked like a fluffy sheep covered in suds.

Later, I sat with Metal Matt at the park, watching as Brucebruce wandered around, pristine and fluffy, while Sabbath growled and drooled on his leash. I slid a box of cronuts over to Metal Matt. He gave me a lemon-ginger kefir.

He said, Here's to trying to be healthy and yet still breaking the rules. We each bit our cronut and then sipped the beverage.

You keeping Brucebruce? he said.

I don't know. Can you *keep* anything really?

You can keep a dog, my friend.

I guess. If he wants to stay.

That's sweet. You clearly care for him. In fact, what happened? His coat is so clean.

We took a shower.

Together?

Obviously.

Metal Matt laughed. Listen, it's okay to love something.

I looked at Brucebruce, off leash and twenty feet away, sniffing the rubbish can. He started licking brown liquid from the sidewalk.

Metal Matt reached out his hand.

I reached out mine.

We touched, and I couldn't remember the last time I'd held hands with someone. It felt so natural and easy. It took no effort at all.

I held on. And so did he. And my dog licked the ground. A couple wearing masks walked by, talking about vaccines. Sabbath growled his friendly growl. And the world suddenly felt healthy and safe and, if only for that moment, so damn beautiful.

Vaccines and the Beauty of Pee Troughs

THINGS WERE ABOUT to change, because California opened up vaccine appointments to the under-fifty community, making all of us eligible. Suzi organized a "vaccination bombing" event at 9 a.m., when the online portal was set to open, so that we could collectively get appointments at the Oakland Coliseum. Metal Matt had the coffee ready, I arrived with cronuts and Brucebruce, Kay and Mike had their laptops open, music flowing, a Bill Withers station, which fit the vibe: casually optimistic, mellow and soothing.

And it worked. We all got appointments the same day and time slot in the early afternoon.

The morning of, we decided to BART there, a first since lockdown. The train ride was somber and oddly defensive: No dancers taking up the entrance ways, playing music, laughing. Few people, not an armpit to admire, no smell to relish. Just cordoned-off seats between riders and silence.

We huddled together, fearful of infection and suspicious of rails and hand-holders, disinfecting ourselves immediately upon exiting. But as we left the station, the crowd picked up, and the energy grew. There was a buzz—people speaking loudly as they walked, laughing—an excitement in the air, which I assumed was for the vaccinations and resulting possibilities, all of it so different than the vibe when the lockdown started over a year ago.

It soon became apparent, though, that the throngs were for an Oakland A's game about to begin. Crossing the bridge from the BART station to the Coliseum site, we encountered illegal hot dog vendors, handmade signs providing their Venmo info, because no one had cash anymore, and people selling knockoff A's and Warriors merchandise. At the end of the bridge, signs pointed: Oakland A's to the left, vaccines to the right. But with proof of vaccination that day, the A's were providing free admission to the game, against the Seattle Mariners.

Let's go to the game after, Metal Matt exclaimed.

Suzi said, I've actually never been to a baseball game.

Kay and Mike both said, Giants fan here.

Metal Matt and I turned to them in disbelief, even horror.

Just don't, Metal Matt said. Don't say another thing.

❦

AFTER GETTING INJECTED by an eager national guardsman who looked to be about twenty, and waiting the required fifteen minutes in relative silence, hoping no one had a reaction, we strolled up to the ticket window and got a lecture on following health and safety protocols while in attendance.

Metal Matt kissed each ticket before handing them out and said, By accepting this, you hereby renounce any connection to the team-that-shall-not-be-named from Mordor, across the bridge.

Kay said, Despite the horrible clash of literary references in your proclamation, I accept.

We entered the stadium and found that no one was really following the rules, but everyone was jovial, chanting *Let's go, Oakland*. Cut-out plastic images of fans occupied entire sections of the stadium—a reminder of the shortened, bizarre season that Major League Baseball had played in 2020.

But I felt invincible.

Each of us got a beer, day-drinking in the sun, our conversation quick and sharp and playful. I stared at Suzi and Metal Matt kissing—the eagerness and bravado of making out in public in the midst of a pandemic. Mike and Kay tried to snuggle in the uncomfortable green seating. Some knucklehead held a sign saying LAS VEGAS ATHLETICS, and a few of the die-hard Oakland fans threw empty plastic cups at him. We watched as a couple other fans snatched the sign away and ripped it to shreds and then the sign holder got all aggressive, yelling and getting too close to people.

Metal Matt joined the people in our section cheering and booing. When security finally came and escorted the sign holder out, the applause was infectious.

I got up to pee, and Metal Matt and Mike walked to the restroom with me.

When we entered, I was physically taken aback: I had forgotten about the infamous Coliseum pee troughs. Two or three pee troughs was one thing to witness, let alone experience, but twenty troughs spanning about fifty feet or more, running the entire wall, pee trough after pee trough, looked like a modernist design marvel: white porcelain, stainless steel piping, some filled with ice, a couple not draining properly, half-full with yellow water. What a glorious, grimy, certainly unhygienic design wonder.

I said, You have to take a picture of me and the troughs. Trust me, Terrance will love it.

But trying to take a picture with no one else using them demanded timing and patience.

Quick, Mike said as the last person stepped away.

I leaned against the wall, trying to look sexy and humorous at the same time.

Metal Matt barked out instructions: Put both hands on the wall and look back at us.

Maybe I should lie on the ground, I suggested.

Mike said, No, absolutely not. No amount of hand sanitizer could disinfect you after that.

Tell me again why you're doing this? Metal Matt asked.

I said, Terrance's favorite leather bar in the city, the Eagle Tavern. He never stops talking about the bathroom there, how it's the greatest, how it has these mirrors lining the troughs so you can easily peruse everyone's cock, a delightful surprise every time you need to piss.

Mike said, The pee trough is definitely a dying design.

Metal Matt asked, But why the ice?

Smell? I said.

Clearly not working, Metal Matt said.

Mike said, Obviously, for fun. I love peeing in ice.

We all stepped to the one trough with ice in it and started to pee. We shook our hips, creating designs and patterns in the ice—foolish and juvenile and playful and wonderful.

A security guard walked in and said, You're supposed to use separate troughs. It's called social distancing.

Metal Matt snapped: We're a fucking pod. We can piss together if we want to.

The security guard raised his hands like *It's cool. It's cool.*

No one said another thing until he exited, and then we giggled like schoolchildren.

When I texted a photo to Terrance, he sent a laughing emoji and wrote: *Where's the mirror?*

When I texted a photo to Genevieve, she responded: *Next Thursday at 2. I have an idea.* Which made me immediately nervous and excited.

Watching the rest of the game surrounded by clusters of real people and cutouts of fake people and sitting next to my friends, I concluded: This is life, the new normal. The real, the fake, the pleasurable. Everything would be fine.

The Baby

SUZI WAS PREGNANT.

She wasn't showing, and they hadn't told anyone, but I could tell something was up with Metal Matt. He and I sat in the workspace while I read through résumés, looking for a second instructor for Oakland Wilds but dreading everything about the hiring process. I had full classes four afternoons a week with ten children in each, and now a wait list—enough interest to consider hiring someone else.

Metal Matt was hunched over, organizing his records but disparaging each album he examined: I can't believe how bad this second album is, *Vacation* by the Go-Go's. Literally, I'd rather stay working for the rest of my life than ever listen to it again.

I said, You okay? Covid?

I rolled my chair back, trying to make him smile.

And he just flat-out told me: Suzi's two months pregnant.

I didn't know what to do with myself. I moved toward him. I put my hands on his arms.

I said, Are you sure?

He looked at me like *Come on*. He said, Suzi and I are sitting with it, but I don't think either of us planned on this. It was never in the conversation.

I didn't say anything.

He said, I know it might bring up a lot of things for you, and that's not what I want to do.

I said, You never wanted it?

I couldn't help my tone: disbelief, accusation, disgust.

Did you talk about ways to avoid it? I asked.

Of course we did.

If you did, then why the fuck is she pregnant?

Metal Matt stood up quickly.

He said, I'm sorry I told you about it.

I said, First of all it's a baby, not an *it*.

No, it's a fetus. And this is about me and Suzi. Not you and Luna.

You have no idea what this is all about.

I do, Efren, and I'm actually taking this incredibly seriously. Partly because of what you went through and the choices you made.

What the does that mean?

When's the last time you talked with Luna?

I thought this wasn't about me and Luna.

You're right. So, listen, let me make this clear. You have nothing to do with this. This isn't about you or the shit that happened to you. So let that go. You know, a lot of people go through what you did, and it's not the end of the world.

You better think about how you talk to people, Matthew. It's real fuckin' easy to judge someone.

I stood and rushed out of the building, slamming the door behind me and Brucebruce, who jumped at the sound. I started walking, picking up speed until I was running down Fruitvale, breathing hard and fast. Brucebruce followed me at a distance, like he was nervous. Like he didn't trust me or what I might do.

I stopped at Peralta Park. Brucebruce was meandering the perimeter, eating discarded food and other things that weren't good for him, but I didn't care.

I called Metal Matt the next morning. I tried to summon my inner River, to remember his calm delivery, his encouragement to sit with and name how I felt.

I'm sorry, I started. I see how my reaction was connected to my personal traumas and triggers. I wasn't able to listen to you unfettered from my own bullshit. I'm not sure what's going on for me: Jealousy? Envy? Anger? But I love you. And I want to be there for you.

Wow. How long have you been practicing that?

Felt like my whole life.

Metal Matt said, But actually, you storming off kind of helped. I told Suzi about it, and we decided right then and there we needed to figure this shit out. She made a list: the pros-and-cons thing. We discussed options.

Options?

Abortion. Adoption. Marriage. Co-parenting.

What do you want?

I want a drink.

I got you. Anytime you need one, I'm here.

That night, I took Metal Matt out to get various beverages:

kava cocktails, kombucha on draft, as well as nonalcoholic IPAs, moving from parklet to parklet. We both hated them: cars rushing by, the ever-present worry that some random driver might slam into us. I never brought the baby up directly, focusing instead on just being a friend, asking questions about his relationship, about what he believed his options were, tracing fears or concerns to possible outcomes.

Mostly distracting him.

I enjoyed taking care of him, like I was useful and responsible, like I understood exactly how overwhelming something can appear to be. How irrefutable, undeniable. How you can come to believe there is no other way. Because of that, I could provide the space for him to feel all that, to mourn it and hate it and cry into it. And then provide the utter faith that he would get through it, live through it, rise up from it. I felt invincible, like I could care for plants and cats and dogs and friends and everything in the world.

It took them exactly two weeks to make the decision to keep the child.

When he told me, I said, I'm glad you're going to keep the baby. That you're going to be a father.

He said, And you're going to be a tio. But I have to be honest, Tio Chino rolls off the tongue a bit better than Tio Efren.

Who knows, I said. Maybe the baby will choose me a new name.

SO OVER THE next few months, we focused on each other while the world imploded: the proliferation of fake news, Covid conspiracies, variant after variant, mask mandates ending

and being reinstated, indoor shopping opening up and then closing down. Waves and spikes dominated the conversation, but so
did getting back to normal, so did high vaccination rates and
boosters.

But then two things happened: Suzi and Metal Matt broke
up, and I finally got an appointment for a colonoscopy.

They announced the breakup at our Thursday Zoom hangout, which we still did even though we all regularly spent time at
the Fruitvale workspace together.

Suzi said, I want to start by sharing some news.

You're pregnant again, Mike joked.

Not really good news.

In the Zoom squares, I watched the most important people
in my life—Suzi, Metal Matt, Kay, and Mike—stop moving. My
body stiffened. I braced. I studied Suzi's face for signs of loss.

Suzi said, We want you to know that although this is some
big news and things obviously will change a bit, nothing drastic
has to happen.

Metal Matt said, We are separating. But we still plan on
co-parenting.

Kay immediately said, We are here for both of you. I can't
imagine how difficult this must have been. But the last thing you
have to worry about is our support.

I relaxed, my body melting a bit into my chair.

I side-chatted Metal Matt: *WTF. Are you okay?*

He side-chatted back: *Let's talk tomorrow, but yes.*

The next morning, when Sabbath saw Brucebruce at Peralta
Park, he took off and yanked Metal Matt to the ground. He'd
been scrolling on his phone, not paying attention, and the device

shot out of his hand and bounced on the sidewalk. I ignored Sabbath jaunting past me and rushed to Metal Matt, lying in the middle of the sidewalk.

It's been that kind of day, he said, sitting up.

The dogs both trotted back and sat as well.

They could tell.

I said, So your pregnant girlfriend is breaking up with you. Perhaps it's better now than after?

Are you trying to be funny?

Maybe. I'm not sure.

You're not.

Figures.

A person walked by, and Sabbath growled. Metal Matt grabbed the leash and lightly smacked his muzzle.

Do you want to tell me about it?

He said, Not now, but you're right. Better figure out how to do this apart and alone before we actually have to do it.

You won't be the first single parent in the world.

That doesn't really mean much.

Maybe not, but it means you can do it. And you won't be alone.

I playfully swatted Sabbath's muzzle as well.

AT THE ZOOM hangout a few weeks later, we all acted normal. But I was bristling with a new concern: my anus and my upcoming colonoscopy. I knew I couldn't be the only one with questions about asses, so why the social silence? I mean, I understand: generally, people don't really want to sit around sipping rosé and discussing the difference between a hemorrhoid and a polyp, with whose difference I was now very familiar, thanks to my WebMD doom-scrolling.

I mean people should, but they don't. River had suggested I check in with my friends, ask them about their own ass experiences and health, which had sounded like a great idea at the time.

I actually was impressed when I reflected on the subjects we had already broached as a friend group: mental health, therapy, addiction, drinking, breakups, fertility.

However, that night, we went lowbrow: discussing the difference between streaming services.

Suzi asked, Which is better: Netflix or Hulu?

Don't forget YouTube's got options now, Metal Matt said, transparently trying to justify his own YouTube TV subscription.

I examined both of them: their faces, their voices, for some clue to their true thoughts. Metal Matt appeared resolved, stoic, mouth closed up tightly. Suzi had gained healthy weight in her face, the baby making its presence known.

Kay said, Shouldn't we consider library streaming services? They have excellent documentaries, and it's free. I do a lot of research that way for my writing.

Both Metal Matt and I groaned. Kay had begun reminding us at every opportunity of her literary aspirations.

Mike defended his partner, Now, now boys.

Suzi said, Okay, let's do this. Everybody post in the chat all of the subscription services you pay for.

Then she posted: *I bet we all have Amazon Prime, correct?*

Suzi added to her post the typical suspects: Netflix and Hulu, for which again, each of us had accounts.

People posted their secondary accounts: Sling, Disney, HBO.

The amount of money we spent monthly on identical subscriptions was ludicrous. Suzi immediately proposed we consider the viability of collective accounts. Mike and Kay, in unison, though, shot down the Amazon sharing, because shopping histories would be visible to everyone, and that could be awkward. Which immediately made me curious about what they were buying.

I began recalling my own items that could be sensitive or personal or just plain embarrassing. My list included lube, a dozen of those sex-toy silicone eggs Terrance turned me on to, knockoff concert T-shirts, and, recently, an inordinate amount of Preparation H.

Metal Matt broke the silence by suggesting we share secondary accounts, like Spotify or Uber Eats.

But Kay and Mike's admission about their OnlyFans subscriptions blew the evening open.

They confessed to not only following twelve OnlyFans accounts, for a total of $73.99 per month, but admitted to having their own page.

I immediately went to OnlyFans, as did everyone else, and we had a blast reading out loud the profile names and descriptions: Alley Load. Tagline: *What happens in the streets . . .* Apologetic Karen. Tagline: *She knows how to say sorry.* OhNoHesALeo. Tagline: *Let me show you my chart.*

Mike calmly explained, Hey, it's all in line with good politics: We support sex workers and pay for porn, rather than support the ad revenue of massive sites like YouPorn that clearly exploit everyone.

I desperately wanted to hear their nom de plume, but they wouldn't reveal it.

Kay said, And really, what's the difference between OnlyFans and other social media?

The difference is the image of your naked visage, I blurted out.

Yes, but you have to pay to see it, and, really, what you see is up to me. I could just post pics of my svelte feet if I wanted.

And people pay for that? Metal Matt asked.

You'd be surprised what people pay for, Kay said.

Suzi jumped in, trying to rein in the conversation: Look at us and all our subscriptions.

I side-chatted Mike and Metal Matt, *Hey, you two, I need some help. Can you both meet me for coffee soon? I have some personal questions I need to ask you.*

❧

A MONTH BEFORE the pandemic began, my doctor suggested a colonoscopy after I had complained to her about sporadic bouts of bleeding.

She said, It couldn't hurt, and fake-laughed like she'd just told a joke.

She said, Plus, I doubt it's anything.

Okay, I said.

But even if it is, it's very treatable, she added.

But you said it's probably nothing, I responded, feeling less okay about it.

Of course, and if it's not, it's treatable.

Then everything shut down, and I was left waiting.

And I hated waiting, because I—despite my clear

204 | Tomas Moniz

understanding of the statistics and the science that supported her claim that it would be very treatable—believed I was deathly ill.

So when Mike and Metal Matt met me at Red Bay Coffee, the parklet empty, I wasted no time.

Listen. This is awkward, but I figured, Hey, one way to fight toxic masculinity: talk about real things. I smiled wide and raised my eyebrows like *Haha*.

And I paused, because I immediately understood that as close as we were—especially Metal Matt and me—we never really discussed the dirty, messy parts of sex. I felt uncomfortable and vulnerable. I knew my friends were exactly the people I should talk to, but all this shame coursed through me, and then anger that I felt ashamed. I had a surge of rage at River for his suggestion. I was spiraling.

Efren, tell us what's on your mind, Metal Matt said.

I breathed in deeply and just blurted it out.

I'm getting a colonoscopy, and I'm nervous. The doctor said it's just precautionary, but still. Do either of you get like hemorrhoids or blood when you take a crap or after you have sex? I . . . It tends to happen more so after I have sex with . . . well, anyone, even just myself. Maybe I'm just being too rough on the ol' bum?

I said this last part to try and lighten the mood.

Mike's face was one big grin, and he chuckled as he said, Efren, I don't mean to laugh, but ass play rarely has anything to do with hemorrhoids. But, damn, a hemorrhoid can definitely interfere with ass play. I should know. Literally, Kay and I get more requests for her to peg me than any other act we perform.

I almost don't know how to respond to that, I said.

I do, Metal Matt said. What's the most popular thing you do on camera?

That'll cost you $29.99 a month, my friend.

Seriously, no friend discount?

I said, Maybe I should start my own OnlyFans page. To rid myself of this shame. To reclaim my ass!

Mike said, Maybe. However, the more intriguing question: Have you ever filmed yourself getting sexual? Maybe you should try it first.

That night, I followed his suggestion, supplementing with YouTubed directions: Camera angled down, foreground illuminated, a soft white, not the stark cafeteria blue-white. Make eye contact with the lens. No jarring art on the walls, no messy bed or bookshelf in the background.

As I set up the room, I considered account names. Mr. Fiddleleaf was my favorite, but I had some good runners-up: Mr. Science Friday or PuffyButtBikeShorts.

I took out my toys and lube, a pleasing array of choices artfully arranged on the crisp white duvet cover. I showered and shaved and trimmed and got in front of the camera. I arranged my laptop to the side, streaming on repeat the dirty-talking roleplay porn that always got me so hot. Visuals weren't necessary—just the audio of the dialogue, the cheesy commands, the faux-desperate pleas for *More, please, more,* or *Oh my god, we shouldn't.*

The camera had recorded for barely five minutes before I dropped everything to the floor and fell back on the bed, spent and shocked at how quick it all had crescendoed.

Perhaps watching your own sex tape right after satiation was a bad idea, because, oh my god, the video horrified.

I couldn't believe I looked like that.

I couldn't believe it looked like that.

I deleted it before I got to the end.

The following Zoom happy hour subject: returning to indoor bars or restaurants.

Who has done what so far?

I side-chatted Mike: *Hey, thank you for warning me about the video.*

Mike wrote: *It takes getting used to.*

I wrote: *How do some people look so good?*

The others in the group posted names of various outdoor cafés as well as beer gardens they recommended.

I added to the list: *Ghost Town Brewing just opened up.*

Metal Matt wrote to everyone: *Metal and beer.*

Then Mike side-chatted: *Practice leads to confidence.*

Kay added to the group chat: *I love all the parklets. I do a lot of my writing in them.*

I wrote to Mike: *I'm pretty confident, but my god . . .*

And then I saw in the group chat: *Efren, you clearly aren't that confident about your ass, and that's okay.*

On the screen, sure enough: everyone is smiling.

Suzi said, I think someone's private chat accidentally went public.

Metal Matt fake-screamed.

Mike said, I'm so sorry, everyone, but, yeah, Efren and I were discussing the art of filming yourself, and we are not embarrassed.

For a second: just awkward expressions in little Zoom squares.

Kay, bless her heart, suddenly posted the party popper

emoji. She raised a glass and said, Here's to Efren's ass and his confidence.

Suzi, without missing a beat, said, Now that would make a great OnlyFans username: Efren's Confident Ass.

And she was right, because it was already taken.

Breathless but Ready for Anything

EVERY OAKLAND WILDS class ended with a sappy little song and a litter pickup. *Clean up, clean up, everybody clean up,* I'd sing, maybe also clap a couple times, and the kids, mostly ten-year-olds, would shrug and groan and retrieve a trash picker upper.

I didn't believe that that was actual name of the tool, but it was.

I discovered this when I Googled the clawlike device, because of something Suzi had asked.

Suzi said, as we stood in the kitchen of the workspace one morning, Have you considered what they might pick up in Dimond Park? How might a parent react if Little Sarah's hand had touched a condom or a needle?

Mike raised his eyebrows like *Oh damn.*

He said, I'm no parent but I'd be pretty disturbed for Little Sarah.

It was a weird moment, and I was struck with a wave of sadness, quickly followed by a sense of shock, disbelief. I hadn't considered how a parent might react.

I hadn't thought twice about it because—it was true—I wasn't a parent.

I overnight-shipped ten trash picker uppers to my apartment.

Along with the plant life my students and I discovered in the park—redwoods, giant sequoias, stately Italian stone pines, a couple California buckeye trees, plus Shumard red oaks, southern live oaks, and American elms—we started a running list of the most interesting discarded discoveries: so far, a one-hundred-gallon aquarium with all the rocks and coral still set up inside, two vacuums, one and a half toaster ovens, and twelve mattresses, which the students wanted to jump and bounce on. (But I put my foot down, because now I *have* considered.)

Today's discovery: an infant car seat still in the box. I texted Metal Matt a picture: *You want?*

His response: *I'm gonna need my own. Suzi already has one. So yes.*

Metal Matt had been sleeping—illegally, of course—for the last week in the workspace, because, although Suzi and he still lived together, still were on good terms, that didn't mean they always wanted to be around each other, that the tension didn't sometimes make the situation untenable.

I texted: *You at the office? I'm coming over.*

He texted: *Bring Brucebruce. Sabbath is lonely.*

I entered carrying a gallon of Synergy kombucha and a bag of ice. In the kitchen, I made us fizzy pink beverages in pint glasses with reusable metal straws.

I sat across from him as he leaned back in his ergonomic desk chair, me in my bouncy one, found at Goodwill. The dogs curled up and slept.

I said, Are you ready to tell me what happened, why you broke up?

He explained that it was the most adult thing he'd ever done. Suzi had pulled up some information she'd found on Instagram, like "10 Things to Be Honest About with Your Partner" and "Key Relationship Conversations." They discovered they both wanted autonomy tethered loosely to community, freedom but safety, a home but separate space, a family but independence. They concluded that their best relationship setup was a platonic co-parenting situation.

Instagram told you this, I said.

Insta. TikTok. There's lots of good info there. On Covid. On mental health. On parenting, even.

Aren't those platforms the main source for all the misinformation out there?

Where do you inform yourself?

I guess I don't. I'm willfully uninformed. But at least not misinformed.

Not surprising.

I'm not here to fight. I'm here to check in on my friend.

He said nothing, so I kept talking.

I remember you and me sitting in my apartment in Seattle after you just showed up. No call. No text. Just you. And I really appreciated it. Not at the moment, mind you, but when I think back to all the help you gave me, it wasn't just that you were there for me—it was things you did. You gave me a bike. You helped me meet people. You shared info on places to stay. You never told me what to do. You just showed up.

We sat there, the dogs sleeping, the traffic humming down Fruitvale, the sound of music blaring from passing cars, the BART train in the distance.

What's the plan, then, for you two?

Suzi and I drew up an agreement. I have to sign it and get it notarized. It's all very mature. Though I had to argue that any savings account we create for the baby not be entirely in crypto.

He motioned to his desk.

I stood, picking up the papers, and Brucebruce got up on all fours. I shook my head, and he lay back down. The agreement reminded me of the birth plan Luna and I had made in the months before the end. I perused the pages: home birth, cutting the cord, no plastic baby toys, sections on living arrangements, collective savings accounts, dietary choices, education, including after-school classes.

Just FYI, Oakland Wilds is open to barter and/or trade payment options.

He nodded, not really reacting.

I said, Let's go to my place. I made up the living room for you.

And for the next couple weeks we roomed together, navigating the small space with each of us and the two dogs. Thankfully, my basement apartment's best redeeming quality: the glass door opens onto a backyard overgrown with nasturtiums and hydrangeas and a patch of red raspberries I planted. We'd each purchased those foldable beach chairs with straps so we could walk up to Peralta Park and set them out during the height of the pandemic. Now we arranged them in my yard beside the old wooden Adirondack chair, facing west, toward the sunset, plus a reclaimed Ikea footstool in between to place our beverages on. I did morning poop duty, he did evening. I did coffee: mine, black, his, with one small spoonful of honey for medicinal purposes. He did evening beverages: usually some new (and awful, to be honest) sour beer or a natty wine, which made me want to gag (the name, not the flavor, which I kind of enjoyed—funky and footy).

Until one morning, a knock on the door made Brucebruce stand. Never one to bark, Brucebruce looked at me, ears up like *You gonna answer that?* and I shrugged. I waited for the second knock, sipping my coffee, enjoying the time Metal Matt wasn't home, glad that his job setting up sound for events had picked up again despite the ever-present Covid surges.

It was Jan, from upstairs, holding Balls.

Hey, Chino.

It's Efren, I said.

Sorry. Ugh. I'm just so upset.

She started crying, and I was impressed at the ease with which the tears flowed.

I didn't know what to do with my hands, but I knew what to say: Are you safe? Do you need me to call someone? Come in.

She shook her head no and said, I'm sorry. My mother. She's sick. Covid. She's . . . I need to go home. Jas and I hoped we could make you an offer if you watch the cats. I know you took care of them when they ran away—I don't know if we ever properly thanked you.

Balls yawned, and I remembered his velvety, round testicles.

How's Ratty?

She snorted. And then sighed. We call her Cobain. But it's

funny you say that because Jas calls her a *fat rat bastard* in some Scottish accent. I think it comes from a movie.

I say, *Austin Powers.*

That's the one.

The deal: Watch the cats, water the plants. In return, I could stay in their two-bedroom apartment if I so wished while they were gone—approximately a month or so—and I could use their Peloton as well. Jas even provided me with a brand-new pair of bike shorts with the padded ass.

I'm a sucker for good houseplants, but I worried about Brucebruce being jealous. Ultimately, I reasoned that if he could choose to stay with me unleashed, he could deal with a couple cute cats. In fact, I'd come to believe that Brucebruce had decided I was his person. I still regularly reminded him that he could go anytime, that he was free. He never took me up on the offer.

Plus, the arrangement meant that Metal Matt and Sabbath could stay in my place and spread out a little.

After Jas and Jan left for the airport, the cats played at my feet, and I felt the soil of each plant in their apartment, noting that the ficus had definitely been overwatered. The stationary bike sat in a little breakfast nook turned exercise room. I hadn't really worked out since the spin class the summer we fought the Nazis.

I remembered the storage locker in Seattle. The boxes I placed in there, unwrapped, for our baby. That was the last thing Luna had written to me about: our contract with the storage company. I'd never responded. I simply ignored the message, because how could I deal with it? I knew Metal Matt and Suzi could use all the baby stuff, but that would require me to call Luna. I wondered if that was necessary. But immediately I knew it was—it was something I should have done a long time ago.

I explored the packaging of the bike shorts for directions, feeling ridiculous, but nevertheless a bit disappointed not to find some clarification or guidance. *Do you wear underwear with them or not?* I texted Mike. I needed to know.

He texted: *Always underwear. That's a life lesson. Me and Kay will stop by tonight.*

I got on the bike, ready to get healthy.

At my last video medical checkup, reviewing my stats (weight and height) in preparation for my upcoming colonoscopy, my doctor acknowledged that although BMI was malarky (her word), that didn't mean you don't want to pay attention to the amount of strain you are placing on ankles and knees and hips.

She asked, How do you want to move around the world when you're fifty and sixty and seventy and ninety?

It was a specific question about the quality of life as you aged, but the question gnawed at me: How do I want to be able to move through the world?

I scrolled through the Peloton classes: sorted by musical genre, by decade, even by band—an entire class devoted to Metallica. I thought of Metal Matt and pressed START. Maybe it was the strangeness of being the only one in this little kitchen, on a bike, with a video of another person also alone in a room on a bike, barking encouragement at me, acting as if this were the most natural thing in the world: being alone together in our separate spaces.

But I loved it. The teacher wore makeup and jewelry and had fancy spandex attire. Her fake-blond hair swinging wildly, she admonished me to ride hard, to not give up, to lean into the difficulty, the pain, the work. It was the greatest twenty-minute class, and at the end I was drenched in sweat.

Brucebruce stared at me from the next room, the cats nowhere to be seen. I felt breathless but ready for anything, thinking that I knew exactly how I wanted to move through the world.

I was sitting in the backyard, still sweating, with Brucebruce in another chair, Ratty in my lap, and Balls sprawled in the grass, when Metal Matt returned home with Sabbath, cradling a bag of groceries.

Sabbath immediately yowled and tried to bound toward the cats. His slow growl was more playful than serious, but the cats bolted, and Ratty scratched my thighs and forearm in her escape. It didn't matter, though, because I felt strong and powerful and able to heal.

I said, I got some crazy good news. I mean, it's a little sad, because I love sharing a studio apartment with you, I do, but I'm moving out.

Metal Matt's face fell, and I regretted my joke.

I added, Upstairs. The people upstairs had an emergency, and they asked me to stay there for the next month. But the best news is they have a Peloton, so we can work out. Have you seen the music list? I've got to show you.

I was scrolling through the class list with him when Kay and Mike showed up with three different four-packs of beer: a regular IPA, a gluten-free pale ale, and a NA hazy.

Kay said, Here's my theory: start with the regular IPA, and you'll never realize what you're missing as you finish the gluten-free one and end with the nonalcoholic one.

Metal Matt said, Point taken, but what if you need to drink more than three beers?

She said, No one needs to drink more than three beers.

Maybe not. But when your best friend says he's moving out on the day you get your separation plan notarized, you might want more to drink.

Kay didn't respond, just grabbed the IPAs and passed them to Mike, who ceremonially opened each one and said, Drink what you want, because, my friend, you now have access to a forty-five-minute Iron Maiden spin class. You can work any number of beers off.

We sat in a circle in the backyard. I suggested that we choose a name for the house, reminding Mike and Kay of In Chan Kaajal, My Little Town, the park in the Mission where we hung out the night we met Leila and spray-painted the sidewalk.

Metal Matt said, You spray-painted a park name on a sidewalk?

I told Metal Matt the story of the brown buffalo and the Mission Hotel. Telling the story felt good, to have memories that made me happy, as well as ones that broke my heart. I was shocked to realize that I had both now.

We each shared stories of what the world was like before: the packed bookstore readings, the rambles to parks and oceans, sharing sips from red plastic cups, being too close to strangers, and, always, how we took all that for granted. The BART cars crowded, the intimate outdoor patios, the standing-room-only concerts, workspaces without sign-up sheets for time slots, hooking up, workout classes, Chinese food lunch counters.

Metal Matt told us about Suzi's doctor visits, which he couldn't attend because of limits on people in rooms.

I said, I can't even imagine . . .

And I had to stop talking. I hadn't burst into tears in a while, but it hit me hard. I covered my face with my hands. I hated being in the delivery room, but I am so thankful I'd had the option, the right.

Kay talked about the patients' rights movements that had sprung up during Covid. She shared a story about how the bureaucracy of hospitals had prevented people from being in the same room with their dying relatives.

Metal Matt said, When I was waiting for Suzi at one of our appointments, I saw about fifteen people crowded around an iPad, crying and saying *I love you* to someone who was clearly not doing well. And this woman walked by and shouted, *You're supposed to be six feet apart.* The group turned to look at her. The expressions on their faces . . . I just wanted to scream at the woman for saying that to them.

Mike said, Do it now.

Kay agreed.

I said, You made me scream on the beach, remember? Your turn.

Metal Matt stood. Then Brucebruce and Sabbath. Mike and Kay and I followed.

Without waiting, we screamed and howled and yelled and shouted, and if there had been a body of water, we would have run into it, if there had been a message missing, we would have spray-painted it, if there had been a group of people mourning, grieving, hurting, we would have protected them.

Tio Flores

SUZI WALKED INTO the office as I printed up maps of Dimond Park at my desk. We were the only ones there. I knew she was extra-cautious about Covid, even more so now that she was getting closer to her due date, so I began packing up to give her space.

It's fine, she said, locking the door behind her and pulling up her handmade mask.

You sure? I can put on my mask too. And I did just test a few days ago.

Then I'm sure you're totally negative.

Ha, yeah, famous last words.

Her pregnant body shocked me. It's not like I didn't know how a body changes, but it was the way she moved as she walked: carrying something heavy and real, something coming. The last few times I'd seen her on Zoom, her face had filled out and she had gained weight in the neck, maybe her arms, but in person, she hadn't put on weight so much as expanded, become denser, more present: her belly taut and erect, rather than round and soft like Luna's.

She extended her elbow to greet me, but I said: Can I hug you?

She shook her head no and said, I have been virus-free so far, so why risk it? But you can kiss the baby. Matthew loves to do that.

I immediately knelt in front of her. She lifted her shirt, a dark line running down the front of her belly. I placed my face on her skin, so, so warm. I kept my face there, waiting for something. She patted my head and then stopped but kept her hand in my hair.

I stood awkwardly and returned to my desk to put a mask on as well, the disposable surgical kind that I had worn too many times already.

She said, I wanted to say thank you for putting Matthew up while we try to figure out our living situation. Did he tell you that the owners of his place are asking us to leave?

I think they can't do that.

They can if they offer a relocation payment, and they did, so it's tempting. I can always move back to Chico for a bit.

I had this fear that if she moved away, Metal Matt would follow her, that I'd be alone again in my studio.

She said, Luckily, I have really great clients. All of them support me taking six months off and picking up my contract after that.

I said, It's not luck. You're very dedicated to your work. I can tell. I'm sure they'll be stoked to have you back.

She said, Thank you. And I've been meaning to tell you: I've noticed how much thought you put into your classes and how you talk with parents. Matthew is lucky to have such a genuine and kind friend.

I walked with her back to her desk, and she sat.

I'll tell him you said that.

He knows. I remind him when we talk and one of us starts spinning out about what the hell we're trying to do. I remind him that he has you.

I felt a bit vulnerable, raw. The outside world suddenly quieted, no traffic noise from Fruitvale. The sunlight spread through the office.

She said, I don't know you really well. But I sense we're a bit similar. I lost my father when I was young. My mother and I have a very fraught relationship, so I don't talk to her that often. I have my best friend, Juana, but not many others. I'm serious about my security, despite doing things a bit differently.

What are you talking about? Crypto is the future.

Trust me, it is. Don't get me started. But here I am: I'm thirty-seven. I never really imagined having a child. And when I did, it was never really with a husband.

That's a problem.

Please, getting a man is not a problem. Getting a person to take risks with you, to do things in a totally different, nontraditional way is much more difficult to find.

You found a good one in Matthew.

I know. But I also see that I found a good one in you too. My child will be safe, cared for. Matthew is going to be a great father, and you will be a wonderful . . .

I waited to hear what she might call me, to name what I might become.

Instead, she asked, Have you decided how you want the child to address you?

And for the first time, I thought about it, about who I might be, and it seemed so obvious.

I said, I think I want to be called Tio Flores.

Signed at Casa Wildflower

JAS AND JAN called one morning in September with an offer. The deal: I'd agree to give a home to their cats, take on their yearlong lease, and buy their Peloton for $500, in exchange for packing up their apartment, getting a storage locker, and shipping a few things. I told them I'd have to think about it for a night. I felt guilty, like I might be taking advantage of their situation, but they stressed it would really help them to have this wrapped up.

I was fighting a slight cold, my body a bit run-down, so I wanted to take a test to make sure I wasn't Covid-delusional. The test was negative, but that night I tossed and turned, thinking of writing *kitchen*, *bedroom*, *glass*, *fragile*, on a thousand boxes. I had moved so many times just in the past two years—Seattle, San Francisco sublets, Guerneville, Oakland—putting things in boxes, stacking boxes on boxes, moving boxes from one spot to another, the smell sharp and tart of cardboard, that crackle of tape.

I woke in the morning with Brucebruce and Ratty and Balls all side-eyeing me, waiting to be fed.

I petted each of them. I fed them.

I texted Jas and Jan: *I'll do it.*

I walked outside with my coffee, heading to the stairs leading to the backyard, and left the door open. I'd worked hard to keep the cats inside the house. Ratty bolted ahead of me and froze in the middle of the raspberry bushes. Balls hovered at the door, unsure what to do.

I said to both of them, You have a home here if you want it. Just stay safe, come back, and I'll feed you.

They both returned that evening around dinnertime when I rattled their food bin.

I figured the animals and I had an agreement.

And then it hit me. I couldn't believe I hadn't considered it before.

I SUMMONED BOTH Metal Matt and Suzi to the apartment with a cheesy text written in complete sentences and correct punctuation.

When they arrived, I brought out mint tea, brewed with mint gathered from the backyard.

A garden's nice, right? I said.

They both nodded, like *I guess.*

It's good for your health. You can grow things. A baby would love it too.

Do you need encouragement to grow a garden? Suzi asked.

Then I just blurted it out: The people upstairs are moving
back east and offered the whole place to me. The two of them
could move in—Suzi, downstairs, me and Metal Matt, above. I
could help with the baby. I could tend the garden, and we could
have an endless supply of herbal teas. Think of the strawberries
for the baby.

I left them alone in the backyard so they could talk. I texted
Genevieve and asked when she would be back in town.

She always responded promptly: *Next Tuesday. Free from
4–6.*

She was not into texting banter, but I tried to entice her: *Can
I kneel in front of you and kiss your belly?*

She texted: *We can talk about it next Tuesday from 4–6.*

A week later, Suzi agreed to move in, but before anything
happened, she proposed a State of the Baby meeting at the compound (her word for the backyard) so all of us could develop
cohabitation agreements.

Can we not call it a *compound*, I said as we settled into the
backyard.

I kind of like it, though, Metal Matt said as he balanced
three OBGs: his mocktail concoction of orange bitters, finely
grated ginger, and sparkling water over ice.

He said, It's like Metallica and their San Leandro compound,
a magical home that the most divine music originated from.

None of us are musicians.

Suzi said, Speak for yourself.

In tandem, Suzi started to drum her fingers on the table holding the drinks. Metal Matt did the same, mirroring her rhythm
and bobbing his head a bit. I watched them making these faux
jazz faces, as if they were enraptured by the musical creation

deep in their souls. I joined in, because why not? They were both in a good mood: Metal Matt was getting a nice little payout for moving, and they didn't even have to pack everything up, since part of the deal was that the owner provided a moving company.

I said, We need a name that captures the vibe. Like the Nest?

Too creepy, Suzi said.

How's the Garden?

Too religious, but I do like the nod to the yard, Metal Matt said.

I said, It's really just nasturtiums and California poppies and a bunch of wildflowers.

Suzi said, So let's agree to keep considering house names. Now, I've added some changes to the initial birth plan. Some include you as well, Efren, since we'll be sharing space. Matthew, you know I love you, but things will change in the future, and we can't pretend they won't. This child is our creation. Our music. If you want to get sentimental.

She handed each of us a copy and put her hands on her belly.

Metal Matt leaned forward and started reading.

We have just over a month to handle this, Suzi announced, like she was trying to be as clear as possible about the seriousness of the situation.

The addendums to the initial birth plan included contingencies for new relationships, for vacation possibilities, for financial emergencies, for loss-of-life decisions. Suzi and Metal Matt spent over an hour going over personal agreements, during which I puttered in the garden or the second-floor apartment. They called me back whenever my presence was required: usually involving housing responsibilities.

As we wrapped up, she asked, So have you two discussed a plan between yourselves yet?

Metal Matt tossed the pages to the ground and stood up.

What are you talking about? We don't need a fucking agreement. We're best friends.

She said, Exactly. Which makes it so important to be as transparent as possible right at the start. This is a person with whom you are planning on sharing a home with our child. What are your expectations? What are his? Can he bring home strangers? Can he pick the baby up and drive her places? I know you both are friends, but now you're also partners.

Suzi gathered all the papers while Metal Matt and I just sat there. I hadn't thought of any of it. I looked at him, and he simply left and went to his room. Metal Matt didn't come back out the rest of the night.

☙

THE NEXT EVENING, I worked out on my Peloton to a sing-along ride featuring all-women rock: Joan Jett, Tori Amos, the Go-Go's. I tried to belt out the lyrics to each song along with the instructor (who never once got winded), but I simply couldn't keep it up. All three animals were in the room with me, lapping water occasionally, as if they were thirsty just watching.

The ride ended with Hole's song "Asking for It," and the instructor congratulating us for persevering when things got hard, when we struggled up the physical and metaphorical hills.

I deeply appreciated the encouragement, but all I could think about was singing the song wildly in front of Courtney Love the night I met Metal Matt all these years ago.

Still dripping, I moved to the backyard, to feel the cool outside breeze.

I completely freaked out when I encountered Metal Matt sitting there alone in the dark, Sabbath curled at his feet.

I said, Fuck, dude, make yourself known, and threw my sweat towel at him.

He picked it up and held it.

Gross. This is soaking wet.

Emma Lovewell knows how to ride a motherfucker.

You wish.

I do.

I think it is probably against the principles of Peloton to sexualize the teachers.

I think you're right, but damn if it's hard not to when they get all sweaty and their bodies move up and down and back and forth. It's like this massive androgynous lovefest.

He threw the towel back at me.

I knew he was worried about all the things coming. I wanted to pick him up or shake him or hug him or make him laugh.

I smelled my towel and said, I've always wondered why sex with women smells different than sex with men.

Body parts, I imagine. Metal Matt said.

I mean, okay, yes—the obvious answer.

And people. Each person smells different.

Again, yes. Maybe I was being more philosophical than physical.

Perhaps it's hormones. Like pollen. Like how things just bloom.

Please. Do trees just bloom? I said.

I'm assuming the answer is no, but I have absolutely no idea. You're the scientist, he said.

You're right, the answer is no. I'm not talking about funk.

I know all bodies get funky, but maybe there's some essence, some magical elixir created by the commingling of ass, balls, and saliva that's mystically different from pussy, ass, balls, and saliva.

Metal Matt said, I do love when you've had sex and you're like on your way home, you're in your car or on BART, and you catch a whiff of it on your hands, that sweet salty sex smell.

We fall silent for a minute.

Are you and Suzi still . . .

We have a few times. We didn't much during the middle few months, but she sent me this private addendum to *the plan* as the third trimester began. Asking if I was comfortable with possible mandated weekly pregnancy sex dates because she was hella horny. How are you and Genevieve?

We're good. But we don't touch each other. I miss that smell.

I lifted my arm to smell myself: slightly pungent, a malty sweetness to it.

I smell like a good beer, I said.

Metal Matt said, Trust me. You don't.

Then he let out a low grumbly sound that, at first, I thought was Sabbath.

He said, Am I fucked-up for thinking I can raise a child in this way? Be a father like this?

I wiped myself down with my sweat towel and waited, but he didn't say anything else.

I said, Suzi's moving in in a few days. Your baby's coming in a month. You'll never be ready enough, never have enough, never know you're making the right choices. You just choose. And you're a father regardless.

He said, I'm beginning to hate agreements.

Even the mandatory sex one?

He said, Maybe you should get out while the getting's good, before you're held accountable by our agreement.

I got up. I walked into the studio, to my desk, grabbed a paper and pen, and wrote a note in my fanciest script.

I signed the sheet of paper with a flourish and rolled it up like it was the most important legally binding document in the world. I walked back to Metal Matt and handed it to him. He opened it and read it:

Our Agreement Plan
Between Metal Matt (Matthew) and Tio Flores (Efren)

If you live through this with me, I swear that I will die for you.
~~Metaphoricly~~ Metaphorically.
But you know what I mean.

Signed and agreed upon at Casa Wildflower,
Efren Chino Flores

Metal Matt said, That's a perfect house name.

He took my pen, had me turn around, slapped the paper on my back and signed it too. When he pulled the agreement off my back, my sweat had made the ink run in places.

But neither one of us cared.

Family Chooses You

COVID INFECTED KAY and Mike first.

Mike texted the group chat—renamed from The Five Podsketeers to And Baby Makes Six—*Hey, both me and Kay tested positive. I don't think we were infected when we last saw you, but heads up. Sorry.*

The world wobbled: it was hard not to be despairing, despondent, exhausted. The *San Francisco Chronicle* warned of another surge. Indoor mask mandates were being reconsidered, but many people seemed inured to the spike in numbers, accepting their fate. I even found myself maskless walking into stores, talking within a foot of other random people. Oakland Wilds encouraged masks, but no child could keep them on correctly for long, and since we taught outside, I removed mine as well. We huddled close around dead things or blossoming flowers or sprouting mushrooms.

We saw a gopher snake in the path, and I remembered

walking around Guerneville with Buddy with a *B* and Shawn with an *h*. I thought of my dad and the lizard, the separated tail wriggling where I dropped it, my dad laughing.

I grabbed the snake, and it curled up into my palms. We made a circle and passed it around, gently, quietly, with reverence and curiosity.

I moved through the world with an awareness of our biological intimacy, of the way our bodies shed and sloughed and projected what was inside us, all our viral flotsam: a cough, a sneeze, a ball of spit witnessed flying through the sunlight from a mouth and landing on another person.

No one in the pod panicked. We continued to test and mask, and Suzi isolated herself as much as possible. Metal Matt selected safer sound-engineering gigs—fewer evening musical shows at bars or small event spaces, more daytime corporate meetings and retreats.

I brought Mike and Kay spicy tortilla chicken soup and a bag of oranges to test their sense of smell with; I bought Suzi her raspberry leaf prenatal tea.

I gathered flowers for Metal Matt that would dry and hold their shape and color: yarrow and flowering chives with cute purple round blossoms.

❧

WHEN METAL MATT returned from checking in on Suzi, he sank onto our couch in the living room, rubbing his hands across his face and smoothing out his beard.

How are you two? I asked.

Talking every day: doula meetings, midwife meetings, birth rehearsals. I feel like we're doing more processing now than we did when we were actually trying to be a family.

You are a family.

He nodded and said, I think I'm going to shave this off.

Don't do it. I can't imagine you without a beard.

Don't get crazy—I'm still gonna have a beard. But you know, just the more clean-cut version.

Sounds like you're nesting.

He shrugged and pointed to the flowers I had placed in the vase sitting on the coffee table.

He said, Clearly, you are.

I said, Who doesn't love flowers?

Not me, Metal Matt said, and he exhaled and stood and leaned in to smell them.

They don't really have a scent, I said.

I discovered that.

He moved the vase from the table to the counter.

He said, I have to get to babyproofing this place. Actually, according to Suzi, you and I need to. I also have to set up the crib and the other baby belongings.

Luna was all about bassinets, and the baby sleeping with us.

You talked with Luna?

Not for a couple of years. Have you talked to her?

You two are dumb. And, yes, I told her what's going on for me. I told her that I was going to be co-parenting.

She know you're living with me?

I wasn't when we talked, but at some point, she will.

I walked to the couch and sat next to him.

I said, After finding that car seat, I was thinking of cleaning out the storage locker in Seattle. We've got a few weeks before the baby comes, and there are a lot of useful things in there. Not sure you want any of it, though, since it's . . . Well, it's not even used. But I guess it's dead-baby stuff.

Fuck, Efren. Knock that shit off.

Metal Matt pushed me. He looked at me all serious and not playing.

Well, that's why I haven't talked with her. It's the last thing we have to take care of. Anyway, what would you call it all?

He said, I don't think you really need to go through the locker for this baby. I think maybe you need to go through the locker for yourself.

I said, So you don't want any of the stuff in there.

Metal Matt stood and said, My friend, sometimes you're a fucking idiot. I have too much to deal with to handle your issues.

He shook his head and walked to his room and shut the door.

River elaborated the next afternoon when I told him during our Zoom therapy.

He said, Metal Matt has a point, but I think it's clear—regardless of what he says or believes about the storage locker—that he cares about you deeply.

I said, He's probably right. I just thought he could use some of the stuff, but I guess it's all tainted. It's all ruined.

River said, Maybe your willingness to take care of this, after so much time, shows growth. And you never know, maybe you'll find something worth saving.

⅊

THAT EVENING, I dressed for a date with Genevieve, who had instructed me to meet her at a new rooftop bar in downtown Berkeley. The last time we met she told me, *No underwear.*

So in preparation, I bathed and trimmed my balls. I loved how sensitive they felt against the rough denim of my jeans.

I reveled in the eroticism of the pedestrian and ungendered act of cleaning and shaving and prepping genitals. I could feel myself getting excited, recalling that first moment when you

discover—after undoing a belt buckle or sliding up a skirt—
what a lover does with their pubic hair: how they groom, how
they present themselves. There's an ordinary yet otherworldly
intimacy and a strange camaraderie to knowing what a person
keeps hidden beneath their clothes.

Luna always rotated between well-trimmed geometrical
shapes: the rectangle, the triangle, the square, sometimes an
oval. I'd begged her for a chance to plan some design, but she
always refused, insisting it was her pleasure.

Leila trimmed everything to a short, even length. I marveled
at how her hair grew into her inner thighs and out the top of her
underwear.

Metal Matt bragged he'd never shave off his ginger pubes,
which he swore everyone described as cute and curly. I could
attest to that.

Terrance took great pleasure in his mons Mars, as he renamed
it, a take on a mons Venus, though he acknowledged the inher-
ent and problematic reliance on a gender binary.

I said, I love when you get political about your mons and
your grooming practices.

He said, Grooming is always political. That's why I wax it
clean. So I can feel everything: tongue licking, face rubbing, fingers caressing. I welcome it all.

Genevieve had a full bush, thinning and—as she pointed
out—filling with silver hairs. I'd kneel in front of her in a chair
and brush my way through it with my fingers, flattening and
combing and appreciating.

When I met Genevieve at the bar, she was already sitting at
a table overlooking the city, drink in hand. Generally, when I

arrived, I took her order and returned holding the desired beverages like a gentleman.

She nodded at me to sit.

The server approached and asked what I wanted.

I looked at Genevieve.

She said, He prefers IPA.

He said, You're in luck. We have one keg of Pliny the Younger, which, if you've never had, I'd highly recommend. But each customer is only allowed two. Just an FYI.

Are you serious? You have the Child.

We have Pliny the Younger, he restated like I was confused.

I ordered it and said to Genevieve, When I first came back to the Bay after everything, you know, changed in my life . . .

You can say what happened.

After my child died and my marriage ended. See, kind of kills the vibe.

Point taken. Go on.

It was like my first week here, and I was at a bar celebrating my birthday, and some dude told me about this beer, Pliny the Younger, and this secret way to order it—by asking for the Child—almost like it was a religious thing.

And that's what you did for your birthday: order beer?

No, we ordered beer, and then me and Metal Matt ran into the ocean naked in front of like a million people.

The server arrived and placed the beer in front of me.

I sipped it.

The dude nailed it: the beer was like heaven, divine and sacred.

She said, Efren, and paused.

She turned her eyes away from me, and I knew what she'd say next.

This has been a pleasure. But I can't continue seeing you.

I said, As soon as you said my name, as soon as you didn't call me *sweetie*, I knew something was up.

I hoped I didn't sound too angry or disappointed, because I wasn't. But I wanted details.

Efren, my connection to you has changed. People change, and relationships evolve. I know you know that.

So what have I evolved into?

A friend. A person I care about.

And that's why we can have sex.

Not the kind of sex I want.

I listened to her speak. I could feel my balls against my thighs. I hoped she'd tell me one more time to meet her in the parking garage.

But she didn't. Instead, she told me about her grandchild. She asked me about Metal Matt. About Suzi. About their coming child. I shared with her my idea of going to the storage locker.

She said, You know this isn't your baby, right?

Of course.

You're not the father.

Of course.

You're not getting some second chance. Don't do that to the child. She's not some replacement. She's something new. And how exciting, Efren. How exciting is that.

LATER, I CRAWLED into bed naked, flung the sheets off me, and gathered my pillow in its customary mound. My laptop lay open, awaiting my search command.

Most of the time, I enjoyed "service porn": people being told what and how and when to do something. It wasn't necessarily sexual initially, but it always ended up that way. I relished giving instructions, just as much as I desired to be the one instructed, scolded, corrected.

Regardless of what role I imagined myself in, nothing surpassed that exquisite moment a command went from practical: *Take off your belt*—to sexual: *Spread your legs.*

But tonight, I wanted something different. Tonight, I searched for "helping porn" and "collaboration porn." Up popped rows of preview boxes of people bathing or shaving. The most titillating part was the sentence summarizing the content: *Bad doctor helps depressed mom. Sorority girls wash one another's backs in shower. Best friend helps friend in need* (pictured: young man with both arms in slings).

I watched one described as *Therapist helps two argumentative coworkers solve their problems,* and I came so quickly, so easily and immediately, I was a bit dazed, and slightly horrified at myself. I shut the computer.

Porn, for me, was seductive precisely because it offered no depth, required no responsibility to anyone else, just rote desire. I understood then exactly why Genevieve had ended our hookups: we had moved beyond the stage where we were only bodies to each other.

I dressed in my house sweats and sat in the backyard. I could see the lights of Suzi's kitchen and hear her on the phone with Juana, her best friend, and also her birth partner—something I knew from reading the notarized birth plan.

I had believed family and friendship were something you chose or designed. That you planned for and painted rooms in expectation of. You worked to make a relationship. Hopefully, you found some happiness, some way to be in the world with people who welcomed you home, who would check in on you when things got bad, who challenged you because they cared.

But now, I understood that finding your family and your friends often happens despite anything you choose to do. You have no real control. And maybe that's for the best. You can prepare and devise and court and romance all you want, and sometimes that works. But trauma can lead to family. Accidents can create friendships. The world's randomness. The unplanned-for events of your life. Perhaps it's simply destiny, maybe even kismet.

Because there are friends you strip naked and run into dangerous waters with. There are friends you scheme and conspire and spray-paint sidewalks with. And there are friends with whom you stay sober and eat veggies and sometimes snuggle with. Friends you need to let go and hopefully, eventually, welcome back.

And they're all necessary. All friends are necessary.

Brucebruce ambled over to me.

Ratty chased her tail in the darkness.

Balls sat in the shadows, waiting for us all to come back inside.

Ochre and Golden and Sparkly

METAL MATT SHOUTED, Chug, chug, chug, the night before my colonoscopy.

Under doctor's orders, I had to consume sixty-four ounces of a laxative once every four hours to cleanse my colon.

It was the worst: My belly was distended and bloated. I gagged and wretched and felt so nauseous, struggling to keep it all down.

Metal Matt, though, was having a blast.

He shouted from outside the bathroom door while my body purged itself, You literally sound like a faucet.

He read aloud the colonoscopy preparation instructions each bathroom visit.

Check to see the color of the discharge, he said through the door.

I said, It's amazing how they can find so many ways to not call it *shit*.

Okay, what color is your shit?

I examined the toilet, and, lo and behold, there was no shit at all. It truly was discharge, so I retracted my statement.

They're right. The discharge is clear.

It says it may be yellow in color, and if so, that means you have to redo the liquid cleanse.

Bullshit.

You mean bull discharge?

Dude, I'm not in the mood.

I heard him laughing as he walked away.

I hobbled my way from the bathroom to the living room, where Metal Matt stood holding a bowl of warm bone broth.

Drink up, and I'll see you in the morning.

He woke with me at 6 a.m. to drive me to the appointment. Because of Covid, he couldn't walk me in, so as he pulled up to the drop-off point he said, Please remain seated, my liege, and then stepped out and opened the passenger-side door.

He reached out his hand.

I said, I'm not sick, you know.

He said, I know. I also know hospitals suck. I'll be here for you when you get out.

I stepped up to the automatic sliding doors, which burst open to reveal a nurse in a KN95 and one of those plastic face shields, waiting to take my temperature. I stopped midstep, the door ding-dinging, waiting for me to enter. But I remembered Luna and me in our hospital room, remembering Metal Matt's story about patients being alone in sterile rooms without family or friends.

I turned around and walked back.

I said, Please get me a gooey slice of pepperoni pizza. And guacamole and chips. I'm sooo hungry, I want everything.

I got you, he said, and patted my ass as I moved back toward the hospital.

❧

I WOKE ON the bed in my room, and the doctor beamed at me. He was one of those doctors who know they deal with a part of the body most people don't joyfully talk about, so to compensate he was cheery and playful and had this dazzling demeanor.

He said, You, Mr. Flores, have a wonderful last name and a wonderful colon.

I said, I know I do.

I responded defensively because he sounded so shocked by this pronouncement. I had no idea whether I possessed a wonderful colon.

He laughed and said, It's good to know those things about yourself. I should say, Mr. Flores, your colon was spick-and-span. You are certainly a colon-cleanse superstar.

He tried to high-five me, but I still felt woozy, and so I just kind of stared at him. Not that he missed a beat: he high-fived the empty air between us like that was his plan all along.

He said, I took care of three little polyps, just to be safe, and I recommend a follow-up in three years.

I said, I thought it was normally every ten.

He said, And deny me the chance to examine that fabulous colon again? Plus, it's better to err on the side of caution. You never know what the future holds.

I couldn't tell if he was trying to be funny, with his face

masked and bespectacled, his hair hidden away by a medical cap.

But I laughed, mostly with relief, at the knowledge that I wouldn't have to cleanse again for three years.

Metal Matt and Suzi thought it was hilarious.

They oohed and aahed over the pictures the doctor took of my colon. Even admired the polyps, which were printed up in the postprocedure handout. They concurred with the doctor's pronouncement: I was Efren with the Wonderful Colon.

⁂

BUT THE NEXT day, life went on like I hadn't drunk a million gallons of colon cleanse and spent the previous twenty-four hours on the toilet.

I had five new learners sitting in a circle while Brucebruce lounged in the shade of a nearby invasive eucalyptus grove. The word *kids* had begun to feel too dismissive to describe my students. I was trying to show them I was irritated without expressing anger. Every new class eventually has a moment like this: the don't-hurt-the-plants lecture.

I had asked my learners to find some sticks, which, I should have known by now, usually leads to one of them destroying a bush or a blooming flower. In this case, it was two brand-new learners—Sheila and Asad—viciously swatting the heads off a cluster of calla lilies.

I said to the circle, We will do a lot of things here in Dimond Park, but one thing we never do is uproot or step on the plants, animals, or insects that are trying to survive here.

I wanted to be serious without shaming them for not understanding how things depend on each other. I know *adults* who should know better and don't. Sometimes *I* should know better and don't.

I could tell that their enthusiasm was waning, so I added, Now this doesn't mean we won't discover some cool stuff. There're fire ant colonies that we'll watch swarm over bits of food. Sometimes, we'll find dead animals out here. And there are infinite mushrooms and ferns to carefully examine.

I explained that we were going to walk along Sausal Creek, which runs through the heart of the park, as we headed to the Magical Fern Grove—my name for an area full of goldback and silverback ferns. But then, I noticed Suzi strolling by herself, her pregnant body toddling across the grass.

I waved her over, and she paused as if deliberating.

I didn't want to leave my learners to run over to her, so I decided to give her space to decide.

Brucebruce took off, looking for Sabbath, but ended up sauntering up to Suzi.

She walked him back over and paused in front of me. I was shocked to see her without her handmade mask. I asked the learners to hypothesize in their Dimond Park Wilds Discovery Journals: What would they like to discover if they could discover anything? Dropping their sticks, they set to scribbling.

I asked, Are you okay?

She shrugged and said, Not really. Just got off the phone with my mother. She's not going to make it to the birth. She also felt the need to inform me that she thinks what Matthew and I are choosing to do—the co-parenting—will only hurt the child. Only make the child hate us.

I could see the anguish in her eyes, the way she was trying to suck her body into herself, heavy with shame or disappointment or sadness. She didn't say anything else, and I didn't push it—because what would be the point?

The two of us stood in silence.

I said, Come with us for a minute. We are on the lookout for the Magical Fern Grove. We might need your help.

Suzi smiled and said, Some magic might be nice right now.

The learners tucked their journals into their packs, and we all strolled along the creek bank until we found the shady bend where ferns abounded.

The learners and I bent down around this wonderful mature plant—fronds big and arching, a vibrant green. Give me your arm Suzi, I said. Everyone, watch how I do this without hurting the frond. Suzi knelt slowly, holding her belly with one hand.

I made sure to make eye contact with each child, but especially with Sheila and Asad.

I held Suzi's arm and placed the underside of the frond to the inside of her forearm, gently applying pressure.

I said to the learners, Now help me blow on it.

And we all leaned in and blew softly, up and down her arm.

Do you need to do that? she asked.

It's part of the magic.

When I carefully pulled the fern away, a print of the frond and all its spore pods remained on her skin, cradled in the crook of her arm: a delicate outline, ochre and golden and sparkly, with a lovely pattern of dots.

Suzi stared at it like she had never seen something like it. A few of the learners shouted *Dammmn,* and they darted in every direction to grab their own ferns and apply the fronds to their exposed skin.

Who taught you to love plants like this? she asked.

I said, My mother. And, well, my father too. Each in different ways. They didn't teach me about plants, really, just about what it takes to care for something.

No, Asad. Not on your face, I called.

Suzi laughed out loud like that might be the funniest thing anyone ever instructed a child. She said, Efren, it must be so wonderful to be constantly reminded of joy and ridiculousness.

She stood and breathed out audibly. She rolled her shoulders back like she had finally made her decision.

She said, I know you didn't have perfect parents—I mean who does, right?—but to have parents who believed in you, that's a good thing.

I wanted to explain: *My parents were selfish and distracted and sometimes mean and always hustling and angry because they always had to hustle.*

But Suzi was right: they also believed in me.

In their selfish and distracted and sometimes careless ways, they loved and believed in me.

You are going to be a wonderful parent, I said.

Thank you.

But don't think for a second your child won't hate you a little bit.

Or even a lotta bit.

Even that.

Grieving Is a Thing No One Teaches You How to Do

LUNA PICKED UP on the third ring. I sat in the backyard in the late afternoon and watched the Japanese maple in the neighbor's yard flutter in the breeze. Ratty bounced after a buzzing insect, paws clapping soundlessly in midair.

Chino Flores. I wasn't sure I would answer, to be honest, when I saw it was you. But I'm—Wait . . . Is everything okay?

Yes, yes, everything is fine. I'm sorry to randomly call. I should have texted. But do you have a minute to talk?

She waited to respond, and I could feel my body tense, like it was bracing for something. Like I was ready to react, to fight back. And I hated that feeling in myself, how easily it had appeared, how comfortable it made me feel.

She said, Let me get back in my car, Chino. Hold on a second.

I said, I actually use Efren now.

I heard keys jangling and the beep-beep of unlocking doors.

She said, I always loved your birth name. Since when?

Since my father passed away.

Oh no. I'm sorry . . . I . . . Hmm.

I could hear that she didn't know how to respond. I was angry at myself for telling her about my father a minute into our conversation. The last thing I wanted to do was talk about death.

I'm the one that's sorry, Luna. I didn't want to start like this, but I'm sorry. I'm sorry.

I wanted to say more, but I just kept repeating *I'm sorry*, like it covered everything: My behavior, my calling without texting, my anger and shame, my failure to comfort and mourn and listen. To be kind. To stay in touch. Grieving is a thing no one teaches you how to do. It's a process. It's living through it, and it's running away from it, and dismissing it and reliving it and returning to it again and again. Grief is bodily, internal, a weight you bear continually, something you can't shed, something you learn to live with, make room for. The image of your wife holding the grayish body of your stillborn child, your mother shrinking away in a hospital bed, the declined call from your father the last time he tried to reach you.

She said, in this quiet yet definitive way: Efren, I can't really help you with this.

Of course. I know. That's not what I'm calling about. Luna, I know I should have taken care of this a while ago, but I was thinking now might be a good time to clean out the storage locker. Would you want to do this with me? No pressure at all.

Pressure? I don't feel pressure. I feel . . . I don't know . . . I feel stunned, or just like . . . Really? Seriously? Like *you're* ready now, and so you want to see if *I* want to do it with you. As though you're being generous or kind.

I said, Luna, I was afraid. I didn't want it to be real. I feel like I'm still holding on to all of it, that I'm just figuring out how to put it down.

Put *him* down. Our baby was a boy, and you never even wanted to hold him. You didn't want to talk about him—as if he never existed. But now you want to go through the baby things. *Now* you want to process all that with me.

I said, I know our baby was a boy.

And as I said it, I felt my body give in, release something.

I said, I really don't want to process anything about this, but I'm also not willing to hide from it anymore. I'm sorry that I didn't understand that at the time. I'm sorry you've had to wait for me. To do all of that on your own without me.

Neither of us said anything else for a while. I held the phone in my lap. I could hear the Japanese maple rustling. I listened to her breathing. I closed my eyes.

&

THREE DAYS LATER, I flew up at ten in the morning, checked into an inexpensive, generic hotel off 99, just east of Sea-Tac. I Ubered to the storage locker and sat outside, waiting for Luna to arrive.

She drove up in a sunshine-orange Subaru Crosstrek.

Don't say a word, she shouted out the window.

I don't need to say anything. Your car says it all.

She walked up, and we awkwardly bumped elbows, then hugged without even asking. We both lunged into each other. And I held her, and I let her hold me. It felt so comforting to see her, still sporting an oversized sweater with a pair of dress slacks and nice leather shoes. She smelled the same: something piney, something flowery.

Neither of us said anything sharp. We stood in front of the locked storage container for over an hour and laughed like survivors, like nothing could hurt us, filling each other in on lovers and jobs and where we lived and how we'd found joy.

Which led her to explaining the choice of paint for the car.

She said, Every single time I walk up to it, I grin ear to ear. All that color. It makes me forget the gray and the cold and the rain.

Makes perfect sense, I said.

And with that, she unlocked the storage door, and we began the work. We started with the larger pieces of furniture that Metal Matt and I had haphazardly shoved in the day before we drove to the Bay: a dresser, a few end tables, a rocking chair. We unwrapped boxes and created separate piles for donation and trash and recycling. We shared memories of how we'd planned to parent: How she didn't want anything pink or blue, especially not clothes. How I was adamant about cloth diapers rather than disposable ones. We laughed at how naïve we were, how hopeful. We sat cross-legged right next to each other, knees sometimes touching, and went through everything.

Remember how I didn't want any plastic toys, only wood? Luna said as she sat and picked through a couple gift bags.

Um, no offense, but there were sooo many things you didn't want, I said.

Hey, I seem to remember you agreed with it all, she said, and she squinted her eyes at me—a gesture she only did when she was serious. She held me in her gaze, and I remembered exactly why I had "agreed with it all."

I said, Of course I did. You were so sure. How could I not agree with you?

I had forgotten the memory box until I saw her pick it up.

She turned to face me.

I felt a rush of adrenaline pump through my chest. My stomach lurched.

Is this . . .

Yes.

You never opened it?

No.

She reached out her hand.

I walked toward her.

We sat on the ground in front of the roll-up door, passed around the footprint and the handprint, smelled the lock of hair, read the card that read BABY GARCIA-FLORES in someone's perfect cursive lettering. I wondered if it was the nurse's, Jodi's. We didn't say anything, but just slipped it all back in the box.

In the end, we got rid of almost everything, arranging a Salvation Army pickup of the gifts and most of what we had purchased. Luna kept the rocker after using it throughout the day. She would rock it back and forth, commenting on how relaxing it was, on how comfortable.

I asked, Did we always have that, or did we get it for the baby?

I asked it so directly it shocked me—without hesitating, without considering my words.

She said, I got it for the baby. But I'm keeping it for myself.

The next morning, Luna picked me up at my hotel and we took the memory box to Point Defiance Park. We had agreed on what to do with it.

I had to admit her car impressed: smooth and comfortable. I told her about my truck, that it was a used exterminator's truck and had this yellow stripe running horizontally around the body, the faded logo of a bug holding an aerosol can still visible.

You never were a car person, she said smiling.

Yes, but I feel like you're moving up in the world, and I'm . . . Driving a hooptie.

We laughed and lightly teased each other, and it felt good and familiar. But we fell silent as she parked, opened the back, and took out the memory box. As we hiked, she carried the box under one arm. But soon, I stepped up to her and put my palm on her shoulder. We finished the short hike with both of us holding the box and holding hands.

In the distance, the Mountaineer Tree came into view. It stood over two hundred feet, a 450-year-old Douglas fir standing on the edge of a centuries-old forest of other big firs, hemlocks, and ancient cedars. It dwarfed its surroundings.

We found a small clearing just off the path, shaded and protected from foot traffic, a perfect resting place.

Luna cleared the soft surface debris, and then we dug our bare hands into the forest floor, moist and fecund, so unlike the New Mexican desert, with its cool, dry, sandy earth.

I worried for a second someone would see us and scold us, but no one came.

We both knew the hole wasn't deep enough, but that wasn't the point.

We covered the memory box with soil and Luna pulled a votive and a notebook out of her backpack.

You're prepared.

I'm not, really. But I'm ready.

We each wrote something on separate notebook pages, and she pushed the candle into the loose dirt and lit it with a match.

It sizzled to life, and we both watched the flame flicker and move and then settle. I touched the tiny burn mark on my arm and thought of my father. I could smell something: cinnamon, something rich and spicy, not floral.

Neither of us said anything. After a few minutes, she placed her note to the flame, let it burn, and dropped it to the ground. I did the same thing with my note.

We sat for a minute. The flame burned, and Luna closed her eyes. I looked around, the area so serene and cool and alive.

She picked up the candle and looked at me, and we blew out the flame together.

After, Luna drove me to the airport.

She said, Efren, I think what you're doing with Metal Matt is a good thing. I think you'll be great.

I felt like I wanted to say something to mark an ending for us.

Instead, I said, Text me sometime.

I said, I've missed you.

❧

I RETURNED HOME with a new car seat, the baby board book *Freight Train*, and a Disney brand mobile with images of various characters—Ariel, Mowgli, Aladdin—such an obvious indoctrination ploy, nothing like the black-and-white mobile I left hanging in our old apartment. But I didn't really care; I knew we could make it ours.

I also returned with Covid.

But it actually worked out perfectly: Metal Matt stayed down below with Suzi. Both accepted that they weren't a couple, but they clearly leaned on each other, took care of each other, reassured each other. Suzi cleared out the downstairs apartment, changed the blinds to curtains, got rid of my rug, happy with the hardwood flooring. The only thing she kept: my maidenhair and kangaroo paw ferns.

While quarantining, I cleaned up the backyard, sending Metal Matt to check out a lawn mower, a leaf blower, and a Weedwacker from the Oakland Tool Lending Library. I trimmed the trees and replaced the soil in the two raised beds overrun with oxalis. I walked the dogs. I ordered groceries and beer and even a couple edibles by availing myself of all the curbside pickup options while double-masked. I scrubbed my stove top and the oven. I wiped down the refrigerator. I kept myself busy with purpose: helping ready the apartment.

I set up the car seat in my truck.

I felt fine. The only downside was that I lost my sense of smell—which actually really fucked me up. Coffee was a bland hot liquid in my mouth. I couldn't smell my own poop. I plunged my head into the toilet . . . nothing. I missed my armpits. I continually rubbed them and inhaled my fingertips. I picked lemons and held them in my hands, repeatedly breaking the skin with my nail, hoping for anything citrusy.

A couple times, I Zoomed with Kay and Mike. We discussed setting up the food train for Suzi and Metal Matt surrounding the big date. We gossiped about how we thought things might change for them: Could it bring them closer, or might they begin hating each other?

I asked, Does it make you two . . . you know . . .

Mike said, *Yes* at the same time Kay said, *Not really.*

It was adorable, the way they looked at each other all aghast, like *Oh shit.*

Kay said, Maybe watching Metal Matt and Suzi go through it all will change things for us.

Mike added, For the better, obviously.

Obviously, Kay said.

When I Zoomed with Terrance, he finally introduced me to his partner, Marco—short and cute, with the slimmest little mustache—with whom he'd just become monogamous, a first for him. He radiated excitement. They planned to live in Mexico City for a while and encouraged me to visit. When his partner excused himself, I said how happy I was for them both. Terrance kissed his fingers and pressed them to the screen.

What Are the Other Elephants Doing?

I AGREED TO drive Metal Matt to BART for his last shift, because Suzi was due in the coming days and he wanted to leave his car, just in case—a no-nonsense black Hyundai that had a broken rear window taped up with plastic, which he refused to repair.

Oh, damn, the baby seat, I said as we approached the cab of my truck.

Can you take it out?

I can, but it's seriously like a science project to put it in.

I can just ride in the back.

That's illegal, and you're about to be a father. You need to put aside your childish ways.

True, true.

And we looked at each other. We waited. We smiled.

I broke and said, Fuck it. Get in, lie down, and hold on.

He hopped in, and I took off, revving my little four-cylinder engine down Thirty-Fifth Avenue. I hit the brakes and heard him slide forward, banging against the front of the truck bed. Then I floored it, and he slid back toward the tailgate. I swerved back and forth the whole mile to Fruitvale BART. I heard him yelling at me and then laughing and then hooting.

An hour later, he called asking if I could pick him up.

His colleague tested positive and was symptomatic: fever, body aches, the whole thing. They'd been indoors working together the last few days.

Metal Matt's fever began that night at about the same time as Suzi's contractions.

In the morning, I raced to Target to purchase the final few items for the birth listed on a note he'd texted me from his room: cloth diapers, Depends, pads, a set of I LOVE YOU panties.

Holding the phone in the women's underwear section, I asked, What the hell are I LOVE YOU panties. Like sexy panties?

No, the basic cotton kind. And if they have bright colors, get them. I tease her that she only wears black. She needs more color.

Upon returning home, Suzi immediately had me rush out to pick up Mike and Kay's iPad so she could Zoom Metal Matt into the room. She also wanted me to grab a Coke and noodles, no meat, from China Gourmet, down the street.

I double-parked in front of Kay and Mike's Lake Merritt apartment with Brucebruce in the truck bed.

They both came out with the iPad.

Kay said, Hey, we wanted to just check in with you for a second.

Sure, what's up? I said, stepping out of the truck.

Are you all right? I know you're doing a lot, but are you taking care of yourself?

Mike said, Drinking water, eating, taking care of the animals.

They had a point: When was the last time I fed the cats, the dogs, myself?

I turned to the dog: Are you hungry?

Brucebruce looked up at me like *You know I am.*

Kay said, Come here. Hug us.

Mike said, Here's the iPad, and we'll bring you some food later tonight. But call if you need anything before then.

I drove to China Gourmet and found a parking spot right in front. Brucebruce sat up like he had arrived at home. I remembered the night I freed him, the first week of the pandemic, excited about the future and so freaked out about losing it all. I remembered that moment I thought I'd drive away from the hospital and leave Luna behind. I remembered that Suzi was waiting for her noodles.

I stepped around the truck and looked at Brucebruce staring at me, waiting. I opened the tailgate, and he bounded out, taking a seat right in the middle of the doorway. The gruff Auntie and the younger woman, both in masks, sat behind rows of chafing dishes: orange chicken, lemon chicken, beef broccoli, and numerous variations of noodles and rice.

Can I get a plate of vegetarian noodles?

We don't have vegetarian noodles, Auntie said.

I looked at the younger woman.

All of them have chicken, she said, as if to ease the blow.

I need some veggie noodles for a pregnant woman.

Auntie stood up and grabbed a box and loaded up some

noodles, avoiding most of the chicken and dishing a bunch of extra broccoli and carrots.

Here. Be a good husband, she said.

I looked at the younger woman.

She'll never know. There's barely any chicken in there. Trust me, she said.

Okay, thank you.

I turned and saw Brucebruce sitting there.

Actually, I'll take a small box of barbecue chicken as well, I said.

❧

I ENTERED THE basement apartment. It was dark, cool, some soft music playing.

I said, This sounds nice.

Suzi nodded.

Matthew calls it Music to Birth Babies By. We each chose every other song. No words, the only requirement. It had to be soothing.

And he knew more than one song?

I did have to push back on a couple instrumental metal ones that started off perfectly fine.

Yes, they never end that way.

No, they don't. This one is his.

I listened for a few seconds and then took out my phone to use Shazam—hands down the best app ever.

Shostakovich *Waltz No. 2*.

Suzi sat on her birth ball, big and blue. Her doula would arrive soon. Metal Matt and she had tracked her contractions: still five to seven minutes apart, as recorded on Suzi's phone.

I said, I'm going to check on Metal Matt, and then I'll be in the backyard for a while if you need anything. And my phone's on . . .

She said, Stay. Eat with me. Matthew's sleeping right now.

I plated the noodles, and we stood around the small counter that jutted out from the wall, separating the kitchen from the main room, music playing, eating in silence. She put her fork down and began that little breathing exercise as a contraction gripped her. I put my fork down as well and watched. Without realizing it, I started breathing with her.

She said, Thank you. This helps.

It does? I asked.

Claire, my doula, told me this story about elephants.

Do tell, I said.

At some zoo, this elephant was about to give birth, and so they took her to the back room or whatever, and a bunch of complications all started at once. She became lethargic and despondent, and when one of the keepers called an elephant expert, the expert asked, What are the other elephants doing? The keeper was like, They're still in the yard. So the expert was like, Bring them to her because they need each other. And then the other elephants came in and all laid their trunks on the mama.

Was it only female elephants, I asked?

She said, I don't know, but I don't think it matters.

I reached out and put my hand on hers.

We walked to the backyard, and Suzi strolled the perimeter, circling and circling around me as I fed Brucebruce and Sabbath and Ratty and Balls bits of barbecue chicken.

I went upstairs to Metal Matt's room and watched as he lay in bed, miserable, his hair wild and matted, his eyes full of that feverish glow. Sabbath followed me and jumped into bed with him, stretching out and taking up as much room as possible. I saw Metal Matt's laptop open, a foot from his bed, perched on three stacked record crates. Beside it, an oximeter, an electronic thermometer, and wads of used tissue.

Feeling better?

More like bitter. I can't believe this shit happened.

You're doing the right thing for your family.

I know, but I'm so damn angry about it all.

Just get well. She and the baby are going to need you on your best game as soon as possible.

I still have a fever and chills and body aches. It's going to be like two weeks before I can even be in the same room with them.

Fuck Covid, man. But, hey, I didn't realize you were such a classical aficionado. I listened to your playlist.

Fatherhood changes a man.

No metal, though?

You crazy. I snuck "Fluff" on there by Sabbath.

Every child's favorite lullaby.

Thank you for being there for her. But I understand if you need to take some space or go to work. Shit, I didn't even consider that.

Everything's covered, and I'm good. I'm going to take a nap for a bit, but let me know if you need anything.

An hour later, Metal Matt called, telling me they needed something downstairs. I entered and Suzi was on the floor in the hallway, halfway out of the bathroom, breathing.

The doula said, Hi. I'm Claire. So it would be helpful if you could sit with her while I take care of a few things.

I knelt and watched Claire grab a bunch of towels from the oven and put them in a tote bag.

I took a seat next to Suzi, hair wet and slicked back, in a robe, on all fours, breathing. I saw Metal Matt's face on the iPad. I put my palm on her back and mimicked her breathing. I heard Metal Matt say: You're doing fine. You and the baby are doing just fine.

I stood up quickly and stepped away, a rush of something I hadn't felt in a while: rage and sadness and a desire for something to hurt or blame. I wanted to run away. I'm not sure if Suzi even noticed, but Claire immediately looked at me as I approached her like *Is there something wrong?*

I said, Is it time to call the midwife?

She said, She's on her way. If you can just stay with Suzi, that would be great.

I noticed on the counter a bunch of medical pads and an umbilical clamp and what looked like iodine. I walked back and sat down. I kept rhythm with Suzi's panting, sweat dripping down my lower back. Suzi hahaha-ed again. She squeezed her eyes shut and grimaced. I wanted to reassure her, to comfort her, so I closed my eyes and tried to calm myself, to find the courage to be present with her. And the first thing that popped into my head: Emma Lovewell, my favorite Peloton instructor.

I opened my eyes and looked directly at Suzi and said: You got this. You're doing the work. You're getting stronger. You're almost to the top. You're going to make it to the top of the hill.

Suzi shook her head yes, like she understood, so I kept it up, breathing with her, encouraging her to ride and ride and ride.

The midwife and the assistant arrived, and I backed away. Suzi's best friend, Juana, appeared next to me shortly after, so I slid even farther back to give her room.

Suzi, surrounded by people breathing and moving about her and the blue glow of Metal Matt on the iPad.

I snuck off to the backyard, feeling dazed. Evening had fallen, the temp had dropped, and the sky, my god, so full of stars. By the door: two sets of glass containers containing food and a note from Mike and Kay. The sounds of Oakland raging on like it was just an ordinary night: a speeding car, a siren, a voice calling someone else in the darkness.

❧

I WOKE UP freezing, slouched over in the beach chair, in the yard when my phone rang. Metal Matt said I needed to get back in there. When I entered, Suzi held the baby to her breast, trying to get the child to latch on.

I stood, stunned at the dangly legs and arms splayed out against her body, the legs kicking against her belly.

The baby's head resting gently on Suzi's chest.

Claire said, Matthew suggested you might want to cut the umbilical cord since he can't.

I moved to the mother and child. I swung my face into view of the iPad.

I said, Holy shit, dude, you're a father.

Metal Matt emanated something tender and innocent. Claire handed me a pair of scissors and said, Just wait a few moments. Make sure it has stopped pulsing, and then snip about an inch up from the baby.

Suzi nudged me with her foot and said, I reached the mountaintop.

I said, How'd you get to the bed from the hallway?

I have absolutely no idea.

She looked divine, with Claire and Juana beside her, arms draped across her.

Suzi leaned forward and offered me access to the baby's belly.

I watched the cord, a grayish purple, remain still, the last of the blood from the placenta back with the baby, then I looked at Metal Matt and said, Congratulations.

And I cut the child free.

They named the baby Rose but found themselves in their first parental conundrum: no birth plan directive for how to choose the last name. Suzi was embarrassed she hadn't considered that issue. Metal Matt hadn't given it any thought at all, he said, his face puffy and full of tears on the iPad screen.

He immediately suggested Suzi's last name. Suzi started crying, but she made no sound—tears running down her face. I wanted to leave them alone to figure it out, but I was stuck holding the screen, both of them talking, Claire and Juana moving around, straightening things up.

Suzi offered Metal Matt the opportunity to choose the middle name.

Right then, as Suzi cradled the sleeping baby, over the Zoom call, in the background, the opening drum beat to Bikini Kill's "Rebel Girl" banged into life from the speaker, and little Rose jolted up and then relaxed.

Metal Matt said, Look at her. She's already a little metalhead.

And thus: Rose Metal Chiba.

Rebel Girl

I DEMANDED WE get a piñata for Rose's first birthday. We drove my truck, with Rose sitting in the car seat between us, down to International Boulevard to pick one out, Brucebruce in the truck bed, head hanging over the side.

Metal Matt said, Is that appropriation?

I'm half-Mexican, I said.

Yes.

And Mike is full-Mexican, and he's going to be at the party too.

Okay.

So by proxy, Rose is at least a quarter.

Plus, she is also half-Japanese.

I said, There, it's settled. The real question is how to put raspberries in there without squishing them, because you know how much she loves raspberries.

I spoiled her with all the best fruit, regardless of season or price, and let her eat as much as she wanted. She loved it when I put the berries on each finger and gave each of them a different voice: *No, no, don't eat me!!!*

You know she can't swing a bat. None of the kids coming can.

But we can.

So *you* want the piñata.

Hell yes. You know, my mom got me one for my birthday once—I must have been five or six—and I loved blowing bubbles, so she got all these little plastic bottles of bubbles as party favors. She thought she was so clever and put them in the piñata with all the candy. And, of course, we banged the shit out of that piñata. But when it broke open and all the candy and prizes fell out, we discovered that we'd smashed the bubble containers. Every single piece of candy was slick and gooey with soap.

That sounds traumatizing.

It makes me laugh now.

Moana's "How Far I'll Go" popped up from the playlist Rose Metal's Musical Education.

Metal Matt said, Put on "Let It Go." She loves it.

She loves this one more.

He growled at me. I stuck my tongue out at him. Rose copied us both, growling and then poking her little tongue out at us.

I hit the FORWARD button, and "Our Lips Are Sealed" began. All of us cheered.

At the Mexican market, Rose chose a Goofy piñata, and I blamed that damn Disney mobile I put up in her room, but whatever.

Metal Matt and I sat down in Taqueria Reynosa, and a white lady across the room kept staring at us.

I fed Rose bits of an apple like a bird, because I didn't trust her masticating skills yet.

Plus, I enjoyed the process: the bite, the chomp, the feel of chewed food in my fingers, the eager way the baby received it, the joy on her face after tasting the sweetness.

The lady stood, slipped on a mask, thankfully, and stepped over to us.

You three are adorable. I love seeing men take care of babies.

Metal Matt nodded thanks and said to Rose, Do you want to say hello to the nice woman?

Rose showed her teeth. Like a brag.

And then Rose made the noise that told me *More,* and I bit the apple and chomped and chewed, and my mouth burst with the tart flavor that I knew she'd love, and Metal Matt mimicked her—*More, more*—and she mimicked him—*More, more*—and she opened her mouth wide and I fed her, and she clapped, clapped, and oh my heart, my heart.

WITH SUCH GRATITUDE:
Heidi, Dylan, Zakiyah, Zora, Ella, Dona, GG, and Gabe, as
well as all my extended familia and friends, for holding me up
even when you didn't know you were.

My agent, Eleanor Jackson, for writing me an actual letter
after reading *Big Familia*, my first novel. It's been wonderful
working with you, and my writing has grown so much from our
collaboration.

And, damn, my editor, Evan Hansen-Bundy: Your enthusiasm and encouragement and trust and love of all the messy,
dirty parts helped make this book wildly better. I hope to work
with you for a hella long time.

The team at Algonquin, for all your care and guidance.

And, of course, my writing community here in the Bay
and far and wide: my writing group with Ariel Gore, Michelle
Gonzales, and Karin Spirn. Minna Dubin and the Heart Rage
crew. Genevieve Hudson and the countless Zoom talks, gossip
sessions, teaching collaborations and stage sharing. Thank you.

I am immensely grateful to all the queer and trans writers,
historians, and activists that have enabled all of us to redefine
our sense of self and sexuality and gender. I am an infinitely better person and writer from the work you have done.

And to all my Korn and Hole fans: I apologize for fudging

concert and tour dates to serve my narrative purpose, but hey, any book is better with Korn and Hole references. Forgive me.

I have called the Bay Area home for the last thirty years. I love writing about Oakland and San Francisco and the incredible beauty and diversity of Northern California, and I want to recognize the Indigenous communities that historically and continually call this place home. As one of my most cherished literary role models, Gloria Anzaldúa, reminds us:

> This land was Mexican once,
> was Indian always
> and is.
> And will be again.

And finally, I love letters. Write to me, and I promise to write back (though only if you include a return address!!).

Tomas Moniz
PO Box 3555
Berkeley, CA 94703